MURDER IN THE CARDS: A 1920S HISTORICAL COZY MYSTERY

An Evie Parker Mystery Book 4

SONIA PARIN

Murder in the Cards Copyright © 2019 Sonia Parin

No part of this publication may be reproduced in any form or by any means, without the prior written permission of the author, except in the case of brief quotations embodied in critical articles and reviews.

This is a work of fiction. Names, characters, places and incidents are the product of the author's imagination or are used fictitiously. Any resemblance to actual persons, living or dead, organizations, events or locales is entirely coincidental.

ISBN: 9781087266923

Chapter One

"Any fool can criticize, condemn and complain, and most fools do." – Benjamin Franklin

The drawing room
Halton House, Berkshire

*E*dgar opened the door to the drawing room and stood at attention, looking resplendent in his pristine butler's black suit and striped gray trousers.

Evie noticed he wore a new pin on his necktie. It had been several days since she had given him the gift; a peace offering he had accepted with good grace. Or so she had thought at the time.

When Edgar cleared his throat, Evie set her teacup down and, giving him her full attention, she wondered if today would be the day when her butler issued an ultimatum and expressed his heartfelt desire to return to town.

Evie knew he had not taken the news she had delivered well. She had finally received a formal letter of resignation from Mr. Crawford who, after much soul-searching, had relinquished his position as the butler at Halton House to pursue a long-held dream of setting up a tearoom with his sister in a nearby village. For the time being, Edgar would have to abandon his desire to return to London and remain at Halton House. But that could change at any moment...

"What is it, Edgar?"

He lifted his chin and announced, "The Most Honorable, the Dowager Countess of Woodridge."

A formal announcement.

Heavens!

What could this mean?

To Evie's surprise, Henrietta burst into the drawing room, her pomegranate colored parasol in hand as she came to a stop several feet away and scrutinized the room as if seeing it for the first time.

Evie gave her a bright smile. "Henrietta. What a pleasant surprise."

"My dear Evangeline, I came here in haste to bring you some news."

Knowing this could go either way, Evie drew in a breath and braced herself.

Henrietta held her gaze for a few seconds and then stated in a most serious tone, "You have an admirer."

Evie's shoulders eased down a notch. "I do?" Feeling instantly relieved, Evie turned her attention to organizing a cup of tea for the dowager.

She had feared something had happened to someone.

News about an admirer seemed so inconsequential, she wanted to laugh. However, Henrietta's stern expression required a modicum of gravity. "Do join me, please."

The dowager looked about the room again. "I hope I am not interrupting or, heaven forbid, intruding. You appear to be alone, which is rather unusual. Have you been abandoned or were you enjoying a moment of quiet introspection?" The dowager's gaze fell on the stack of cards sitting on the table.

"Neither... I think. Although... Lately, I have been trying my hand at a few solitary pursuits such as gardening. George Mills prepared a garden plot for me." Evie gave her a crooked smile. "It's my own personal parcel of garden and no one else is allowed to work on it." Evie suspected that had been the gardener's attempt to keep her away from his precious blooms. "And today I have spent most of the morning in the library reading." In actual fact, she had been hiding and trying to find something to distract her from her recent encounter with a new member of their little community.

"I see, you are fretting."

Fretting?

How had the dowager reached that conclusion?

"And playing solitaire?"

Evie gave her a small smile. "How did you guess?"

"Well, you could hardly play whist by yourself. Does this have anything to do with your farewell tea for Mrs. Ellington?" Henrietta asked and settled down at the table beside her.

Evie shifted in her chair. The day before, she had held an afternoon tea to bid the local vicar and his wife adieu as they set off on the exciting new phase of their lives.

Evie handed the dowager a cup of tea. "Everyone seemed to enjoy themselves. I don't believe I have any reason to fret."

Henrietta gave a small nod. "I am sorry I missed it but I had a prior commitment at the local hospital. The school mistress has broken her foot and I have been keeping her company. Did you know she used to be my maid?" Henrietta didn't wait for Evie to answer. Giving a firm nod, she continued, "She came to work for me as a mere slip of a girl and I immediately recognized her potential to achieve more. Some people believe I meddled in her life but one simply could not let her talents go to waste. Anyhow, I digress...Where was I?" Henrietta looked up at the ceiling as if to gather her thoughts. "Oh, yes... I hear Mrs. Sheffield had a great deal to say to you at yesterday's afternoon tea. From what I am told, she took you aside and imparted some instructions on how to deliver a speech."

Evie gave a small shrug. "I'm sure she meant to be helpful."

"And yet, you do not appear to have taken her advice onboard." Henrietta feigned surprise. "Didn't she tell you to inject more details into your delivery? I'm sorry I missed the event. Then again, according to Mrs. Sheffield there really wasn't much substance to your speech."

Uncertain as to how she should react, Evie sat back and nibbled on a cucumber sandwich.

"Well?" Henrietta prompted.

Evie recognized Henrietta's intention to extricate as much from this incident as she could, simply for her own amusement. Had nothing else happened in the village during this past week?

Taking a sip of tea, Evie smiled, "Mrs. Sheffield

wanted a blow by blow account of Mrs. Ellington's history in the village. Meaning, she wished to hear all about her involvement in Mrs. Howard-Smith's demise." A shiver coursed along her back. Mrs. Howard-Smith's death had come as a shock to everyone and continued to linger in Evie's mind…

Henrietta made a dismissive gesture with her hand. "Oh, but that is old news, surely."

Brightening, Evie agreed. "Precisely. I also found it inappropriate and unnecessary to mention Mrs. Ellington's momentary lapse in judgement." Evie poured herself another cup of tea. Looking up, she saw Henrietta leaning forward. Evie took this as another prompt to embellish her tale. "The vicar's wife did, after all, rebel against us."

Henrietta gave a nod of satisfaction and sat back to hear the rest.

Evie pushed herself to continue, "In fact, if you recall, at one point, we thought the vicar's wife might have been the instigator of the rebellion. But, as you said, that is all in the past. It would have been in poor taste to mention any of it at a farewell afternoon tea." Setting her sandwich down, Evie straightened. "So, who is this new admirer you mentioned?" They could at least have a laugh over that.

Henrietta's eyes sparkled. "Oh, it's Mrs. Sheffield, of course. She has decided to take you under her wing." The edge of Henrietta's lip quivered with amusement. "She seems to think she knows best. While she admires you a great deal, she believes there is room for improvement." Setting her cup down, Henrietta folded her hands and invited Evie to deliver the speech again.

Evie floundered. She had no idea how to respond to the news. Sighing, she said, "I mentioned the essentials. Mrs.

Ellington has served the parishioners well, excelling in her role as a leader of the community. Honestly, I didn't wish to bore anyone with too much information. Besides, they were already well acquainted with Mrs. Ellington's achievements."

"You're sounding a tad defensive, my dear."

Fearing she might not be able to control the next words that came out of her mouth, Evie fell silent.

Henrietta leaned forward and patted her hand. "Yes, I know. Not everyone has the ability to deliver constructive criticism. The Mrs. Sheffields of this world don't realize there is an art to it and one must always endeavor to disguise words of wisdom or else risk being labeled small-minded and petty... Even spiteful." Henrietta tilted her head in thought. "Of course, there are times when one must simply be blunt. But that is beside the point. In my opinion, the woman is embittered and resents your position in society."

Henrietta's slight lift of her eyebrow delivered a wordless warning. Evie decided to interpret it as a suggestion to keep away from Mrs. Sheffield.

To her surprise, Henrietta nodded. "Yes, you must try to exclude her or risk falling prey to her intrusive nature."

Heavens! "That sounds rather extreme."

Henrietta lifted her chin. "Some of us are charged with the task of directing and guiding society. Personally, I feel responsible for safeguarding the name of Woodridge. Mark my word, this woman means to cause havoc in your life."

Evie knew the dowager's remark served as a reminder. She too had a responsibility to the name of Woodridge. "What do you think Mrs. Sheffield has planned for me?" Evie had hoped she wouldn't cross paths with the woman again, something she knew to be impossible because Mrs. Sheffield had already joined several committees.

"Well, according to Betsy who used to work at the vicarage and has now taken a position in Mrs. Sheffield's household... oh, and by the way, I believe that is how Mrs. Sheffield came to learn about Mrs. Ellington's rebellious nature. Yes, my dear, she was baiting you. Anyhow, where was I? Oh, yes... Mrs. Sheffield is hoping to steer you in the right direction."

"How so? And... what makes her think I need steering?"

Henrietta tipped her head back slightly and laughed. "My dear, we could all do with some steering at times. You would think she'd focus on her own family. I hear she has two married daughters who reside in London and Mrs. Sheffield is feeling rather bereft now that she has moved to our little village. I had to search my memory to realize she had actually been born here. Now that she has re-established herself in the county, Mrs. Sheffield only gets to see her daughters twice a year." Henrietta lowered her voice to a murmur. "I suspect that is due to her daughters' deliberate attempt to avoid her rather than Mrs. Sheffield's aversion to travel, as she claims. A likely excuse since London is such a short distance away."

In an effort to lighten the mood, Evie asked, "Is there a Mr. Sheffield?"

"Oh, yes. He keeps himself quite busy and is constantly out and about with his estate manager. No surprise there." Henrietta leaned forward and examined the cakes on offer. "These look different."

"They're cupcakes. Otherwise known as Fairy Cakes. Try one."

"Fairy Cakes? So, why refer to them as cupcakes?"

Evie gave her the tiniest lift of her eyebrow.

Henrietta smiled. "Oh, I see. Cross the ocean and everything goes topsy-turvy. They do look quite delectable but almost too pretty to eat. What are those little swirls?"

"Buttercream. I grew up enjoying these treats. My granny's cook is rather fond of Eliza Leslie recipes. She has been using buttercream to adorn cakes for quite some time." Evie gave a small nod. "I had a devil of a time trying to convince Mrs. Horace to try her hand at baking them. She's a stickler and prefers to bake the traditional fare."

"Well, that is a triumph indeed," Henrietta declared. "My cook has dug her heels in far too often for me to make any demands. I don't believe I have ever seen anything so dainty. I doubt Mrs. Sheffield would approve. I hear say she has quite a weakness for fruitcake and rather enjoys preserving our customs." Henrietta took a small bite of the cake and seemed to relish the idea of tasting something that might prove to be forbidden fruit. "Oh, I taste lemon."

"I'm expecting some guests so I thought we might try something slightly different." Noticing the dowager's eyes brightening with interest, Evie added, "They are Phillipa's friends. They wish to write a play and I have put Halton House at their disposal."

"My dear, are you sure that's wise, especially after your recent experience with Phillipa's friends?"

Evie sighed. "Phillipa has personally vetted them. She promises there will be no shenanigans."

Henrietta gave an unladylike snort. "Since your return to Halton House, you have certainly made life far more interesting and, I daresay, you do so without even trying. What is your secret?"

Evie stifled a laugh. Before she could answer, the door to the drawing room opened and Tom strode in.

"Ah, Mr. Tom Winchester," Henrietta exclaimed. "How is life at the Lodge?"

"My lady." Tom inclined his head and sat down. "I am indebted to both you and Sara, Lady Woodridge, for doing such a splendid job of furnishing the house."

"Do I get any thanks?" Evie asked. "After all, the furniture came from the attics here at Halton House."

A month before, Tom had moved from the pub to his new abode on the edge of the estate and, at every encounter, Henrietta had never failed to make inquiries about his happiness with his new circumstances. It made Evie wonder if the dowager wanted to fish for compliments or if she merely wished to make sure Tom continued to be content to live in the area. Little did she know Tom had been hired to shadow Evie's every step.

Even before she had married, she had already inherited two fortunes, and more were on the way. It seemed enough for her grandmother to want to take precautionary steps.

Tom smiled. "Evie. I must have missed my invitation to afternoon tea. Just as well I needed to see you. I have news from your grandmother."

Evie could barely hide her surprise. She knew Tom corresponded with her grandmother who had hired him to be her bodyguard but she had assumed the exchanges were limited to factual accounts.

"She writes to tell me she will be traveling to Paris and then surprising you with a visit. I thought you might want to know."

Her granny... Visiting? And she was the last to know?

"How is Virginia?" Henrietta asked.

"Mrs. Otway-Wells is doing remarkably well and looking forward to the voyage," Tom said. "Apparently, there is to be a high stakes card game onboard and she's rather keen to participate."

Henrietta tilted her head slightly as she asked, "Do you think she will insist on being addressed as Toodles? I managed to avoid it the last couple of times she visited..."

"Most likely," Evie said distractedly as she wondered why her granny wished to surprise her.

Henrietta gave a mock shiver. "You would think a woman of a certain age would have outgrown the sobriquet."

Evie smiled. "Back home, people who acquire nicknames tend to keep them throughout their lives. They see it as a sign of self-assuredness. I have a great-aunt who just turned eighty and is still addressed as Baby." Evie had received a letter from her granny only a couple of days before and there had been no mention... not even a hint of her intention to visit. "Did she say if she is traveling alone or is my mother coming with her?" Evie asked.

Tom helped himself to a cupcake. "No, she didn't say, so perhaps that might be another surprise. I'm sure she suspects I'll pass on the information."

Evie's voice hitched. "And why does she wish to make it a surprise?"

Henrietta patted her hand. "Take a deep breath, Evangeline. You don't see me panicking and I have more reason than you to panic."

"How so?"

Henrietta chortled. "My dear, I believe you have lived

among us long enough to know how we prefer to behave in polite society."

Admittedly, her granny had a bigger than life personality and did not believe in demure conversations or... Well, she didn't really care for subtlety. If something was on her mind, she normally cut straight to the chase.

Evie swung toward Tom and managed to startle him. "Did she give you a date of arrival?"

"Three weeks' time."

"Is that three full weeks or a ballpark figure?"

"Evangeline, do we need to call for a doctor?" Henrietta asked. "You're huffing."

Evie poured herself another cup of tea. "I have other guests arriving tomorrow and staying for a couple of weeks, but what if they decide to extend their stay?"

"How many people are you expecting?" Henrietta asked.

"Phillipa invited three writer friends."

Henrietta clucked her tongue. "Let's see, three guests and Halton House can accommodate over fifty guests. I daresay, an extra guest will not prove to be problematic."

Tom laughed. "I'm sorry to have been the bearer of such ill tidings."

"Oh, don't be. I'll be happy to see my grandmother and you provided us with a distraction. We'd been talking about Mrs. Sheffield and her intention to offer her guiding hand because apparently she found me lacking."

Henrietta gasped. "I've just realized I haven't actually met the woman. Evangeline, please do me the favor of not introducing us."

Evie couldn't hide her surprise. "Pardon? Surely you have met her."

Henrietta gave a casual wave of her hand. "I might have crossed paths with her but we have never been formally introduced. That gives me enough leeway to pretend I do not recognize her."

Tom nearly choked on his tea. "Someone will have to explain."

Henrietta did the honors. "My dear, I am an Edwardian through and through. We know what we are about. There are some customs that must simply remain unchanged. If someone you don't know happens to walk in right now and Evangeline does not introduce you, then you simply behave as if they are not here and if you were to meet them again, well… You just ignore them."

Evie shrugged. "It's one of those silly rules, which makes everything rather awkward for me because everyone seems intent on introducing their friends and acquaintances to me. To quote from a ladies' magazine, there is certainly much to be said against promiscuous introductions."

Henrietta agreed with a nod. "People are generally very loose with their desire to make introductions. How do they even know their friends desire to become acquainted with you or vice versa?"

Before Evie took a bite of her cupcake, she said, "Did you know that no gentleman should be introduced to a lady until she has granted her permission?"

Tom sat back and crossed his arms. "So, I'm to avoid her." He looked at Evie.

"Even if I do introduce you to her," Evie explained, "a gentleman has to wait for a lady to bow her head to him when he meets her again. If she does not bow, the gentleman has to assume the lady does not wish to continue the acquaintance."

Henrietta leaned forward. "Tom, I might suggest you avoid catching Mrs. Sheffield's attention lest she express her desire to make your acquaintance. She might try to fix you too."

Tom hesitated before exclaiming in a flat tone, "Fix me?"

Henrietta shrugged. "You are young and eligible. Yet, you remain unmarried. That might suggest there is something wrong with you."

Evie set her cup down on her saucer, spilling half the contents.

"My dear, are you quite all right?"

"I've just realized. Within three days of being entertained, one is usually obliged to call on the hostess or else risk never being invited back to the house."

Henrietta chortled. "I don't believe that practice has crossed the ocean. Thank goodness." Henrietta took a quick sip of her tea and then cast a furtive glance at the door.

"I think we might be safe for now," Evie said. "It's only been a day since Mrs. Sheffield attended the afternoon tea."

"Yes, but she might not wish to waste any time." Henrietta set her teacup down and surged to her feet.

"Oh, do sit down, Henrietta."

Not bothering to hide her reluctance, Henrietta lowered herself back down. "I suppose I can always just ignore her. Only, do make sure to avoid introducing us." Henrietta picked up her cup of tea and took a sip. Looking up, she noticed Tom averting his gaze. Smiling, Henrietta leaned forward and patted his hand. "Mr. Winchester, we have been introduced and we have both acknowledged each other. That ship has sailed."

Tom laughed.

"Ah, I see. You are teasing me."

Raising his cup, he smiled. "I couldn't resist."

When the door to the drawing room opened, everyone's teacups rattled on their saucers.

"It's only Phillipa." Evie relaxed and helped herself to another cupcake. Since meeting the young Australian traveler, Evie had become fond of her company and had encouraged her to spend as much time as she wished at Halton House.

"I'm sorry I'm late." Phillipa took the chair between Tom and Henrietta. "I was in the village and I got caught up in a conversation with the oddest person I've ever met and that is saying something since I seem to know many odd people."

Henrietta sat back and exclaimed, "Not Mrs. Sheffield."

"Yes. How did you guess?" Phillipa gave her a bright smile and then turned to Evie. "She seemed to know I've been staying with you and wanted me to pass on her apologies for not calling on you today."

Henrietta tapped a finger against her chin. "I suppose I can always claim to have failing eyesight and pretend I don't recognize her."

Smiling, Phillipa helped herself to some tea. "I seem to have missed a significant portion of the conversation."

Recovering from her musings, Henrietta turned to Phillipa, "We were actually discussing your writing friends. What do they wish to write?"

Phillipa brightened. "Oh, they are determined to set a murder mystery in this house. Don't worry. I managed to dissuade them from calling it Murder at Halton House."

"Well, that's a relief," Evie said and could have sworn she heard Henrietta murmur something which sounded vaguely like a suggestion to name the victim Mrs. Sheffield.

Chapter Two

*"The greatest mistake you can make in life is
to be continually fearing you will make one."*
– Elbert Hubbard

News of her grandmother's imminent arrival sent Evie into a frenzy of activity. The timing could not have been more perfect. The more she focused on everything she needed to do before Toodle's arrival, the less time she had to worry about Mrs. Sheffield.

"I think the second menu clashes with…" Evie shuffled through the pages until she found the one she wanted. "This one. It's the same fish dish."

"But there's a different sauce, milady."

Glancing up, Evie noticed the look exchanged between Mrs. Arnold, the housekeeper, and Mrs. Horace, the cook. It spoke of their forbearance fraying at the edges.

Normally, Evie spent a pleasant hour going over the

menus as an excuse to chat with the cook and the housekeeper. It seemed to be the only opportunity to engage them in conversation and ask how they were faring.

How else would she have found out Mrs. Arnold's niece had gained her nursing qualifications and had soon after met the man of her dreams? And poor Mrs. Horace's nephew, who had suffered the loss of a limb during the Great War and had experienced difficulties adjusting to normal life, had met a most wonderful woman and had settled down, recently celebrating the arrival of their first-born son…

Today, however, Evie seemed to be intent on getting every detail right and, in the process, making Mrs. Horace and Mrs. Arnold fret. Had her own fretting become contagious?

"And the dinner service. We must make sure to use a different one every day. How many sets do we have?" When Evie saw their eyebrows wrinkling with concern and, possibly, bafflement, she smiled. "You have both been tremendously patient with me. I know I have been procrastinating over the choices you have offered. Let me assure you, this does not reflect badly on you. I… I merely wish to get everything absolutely right." And, in the process, Evie thought, she had managed to turn a simple task into an ordeal.

Evie knew what her grandmother enjoyed but her tastes could change from day to day.

"I believe stealth will serve us well." She glanced at the notes she'd been taking. "The flowers. Yes, the flower arrangements will need our attention. I think the colors should complement… or contrast my grandmother's preference for earthy tones. Russet. Bronze. Tangerine…" Evie tapped her chin. "Yes, complement. No, wait. Perhaps they should contrast them. In a subtle manner, without competing for attention." Everything had to be perfect, she silently insisted.

Unaware of the housekeeper's utter state of confusion, Evie gathered her notes together and gave a firm nod. "We must be battle ready."

Their surprised expressions had Evie smiling. "I know. You must think I'm overreacting. Trust me, I'm not. Mrs. Arnold, I'm afraid Halton House will fall under my grandmother's sharp-eyed scrutiny. She'll want to know why I have chosen to make the transatlantic crossing to settle here instead of returning home and she will most likely find any excuse to show me I have made a mistake."

"Begging your pardon, milady, but this is your home," Mrs. Arnold said.

"It's very kind of you to say so." Evie took a moment to savor the sentiment. As an outsider, it had taken her some time to settle into her new life and, back then, she'd had the support of her loving husband. She'd had to contend with many objectors to a foreigner taking over the role of lady of the house, but the staff had been surprisingly quick to embrace her.

In reality, Evie knew her granny wanted her to move on. That meant finding another husband. And when, and if, she did that, it would mean leaving Halton House behind…

Remembering Henrietta's remarks about Mrs. Sheffield, Evie couldn't help wondering if the woman would be happier with someone else taking over the role of Countess of Woodridge. Of course, that wouldn't happen for many years as the current Earl of Woodridge was only seven years old.

"What am I forgetting? Oh…" Evie gave a small shake of her head. "The new vicar will be arriving tomorrow or the next day. I think it would be nice if we sent some fresh flowers and a basket of…" Evie looked at the cook. "What do you suggest, Mrs. Horace?"

"Well, I suppose I could prepare something to see him through the first couple of days. Do we… Do we know if he is married?"

Evie searched her memory. "I'm sorry. I am experiencing a blank moment. Perhaps you could also include some basic staples such as some of your lovely strawberry jam or the orange marmalade… oh, and some honey. I had some for breakfast and I believe we will take out another award at the fair this year." She tapped her pen on the table. "While you're at it, could you organize to send a basket to Mrs. Green, please. And include some honey too. She's rather fond of it." She needed the local dressmaker in a good mood. With such little time, she wouldn't be able to dash to London or Paris but she knew the local dressmaker would be able to produce something splendid for her.

Sighing, she rose to her feet. "You have both done a splendid job and you have my full trust and support." Turning, she saw Edgar giving a small nod of approval. He had been present during the meeting and Evie had made a point of placing all her trust in his ability to select the appropriate wines. It seemed to please him no end.

Mrs. Arnold cleared her throat. "Do you have any outings planned, milady?"

Heavens, sightseeing had never been in her granny's

agenda. "Alas, my grandmother frowns upon what she considers to be bluestocking activities." She smiled to herself. Years before, her granny's favorite pastime had been to follow Mrs. Vanderbilt around as she drove along Newport's Bellevue Avenue in an open carriage, nodding or snubbing. The society queen had provided Toodles with endless hours of amusement.

Evie clasped her hands and pressed her fingers until they showed white. She would have to invite some interesting guests… "We still have a few weeks left to get all the details ironed out." Thanking them, she made her way out of the drawing room. Stopping to draw a deep breath, she told herself all would be well.

"There you are." Phillipa rushed up to her, her short bobbed blonde curls bouncing up and down. "I just saw my friends driving up. They're here."

"While your excitement is quite contagious, I'm afraid I'll need a moment to catch my breath." Evie stopped and gazed up at the ceiling. "I can't remember if my granny prefers cranberry sauce or béchamel sauce or… mushroom sauce." Evie brushed her fingers along her temple. "My head is throbbing."

"Does your grandmother always have this effect on you?" Phillipa asked.

Evie gave a slow shake of her head. "No, but the fact she intends this visit to be a surprise has thrown me out of kilter."

"I can't wait to meet her."

What would Toodles make of Phillipa's writer friends? With her granny due to arrive in three weeks' time and Phillipa's writing friends staying at Halton House for two weeks, Evie would have a week to mentally prepare herself. But what if the visits overlapped? Should she add that to her list of concerns?

"About your friends… Are they as flamboyant as the bright young things I recently encountered?"

Phillipa gave it some thought. "They're quite stylish. I hope that offers some comfort."

"Yes, I believe I can deal with stylish." Looking down at her blouse, Evie wondered if she should look at abandoning the pretty flower patterns she favored and consider the geometrical styles that had come into favor with the younger generation.

Edgar appeared from a side door and made a beeline for the entrance. When Evie and Phillipa reached him, he bowed his head slightly and opened the large front door.

"I'm so excited," Phillipa said as they stood on the front steps watching the motor car driving up. "I haven't seen them in months. It will be good to knuckle down and do some serious work."

"How exactly will you go about it?" Evie asked.

"We'll toss around a few ideas. Someone will do the major part of the writing and we can all offer our input and make suggestions."

The motor car came to a stop and the uniformed chauffeur stepped out.

He had a light spring to his step and a scar running from the edge of his eye to his chin. Evie guessed he had served in the Great War.

Three women emerged from the motor car, all dressed immaculately, their clothes a fine testament to the latest fashion and preference for dazzling shapes and bold colors.

Phillipa introduced them. "Zelma Collins, Bernadette

Peters, and Ernestine Wilding."

The three friends burst into a chorus of greetings and remarks about the journey, the weather and the story they had been outlining.

Evie tried to commit the names to memory but her mind remained elsewhere. She had just spent two hours trying to refine the menus for her granny's visit... whenever that might be, and she still couldn't remember which sauce Toodles preferred. The last time she had visited, she had objected to...

Evie bit the edge of her lip.

It would come to her.

Scooping in a breath, she lifted her gaze and looked out onto the park that stretched for several miles. The trees rippled in the gentle breeze. In the distance, two estate workers were overseeing some sheep. She smiled at the easy rhythm of country living. What did it matter if she served the wrong sauce?

With the initial excitement of their arrival mellowing down, Evie smiled. "Welcome to Halton House." While the trio had arrived in a chauffeur driven motor car, Evie noticed they hadn't brought a maid.

"I might telephone the town house and ask Millicent to come down," she murmured.

"Oh, you mustn't fuss," Phillipa assured her. "Ernestine has a maid but she's used to getting by without one when she travels. Zelma and Bernadette will manage too."

"It's no trouble. Millicent will enjoy the trip down to Halton House. From what I understand, she has been complaining of not having enough to do and this makes her jittery." Evie's shoulders lowered. "She's actually afraid she'll lose her position." Since settling at Halton

House, Evie had made no plans to return to London, but she continued to maintain the town house fully staffed.

Edgar directed the footman who were taking care of the luggage and then he stood at attention awaiting further instructions.

Evie gave a small nod. "Edgar will show you to your rooms. We'll be having refreshments in the morning drawing room."

"Fabulous," Zelma Collins offered. "We're eager to get started."

"Oh, then you might want me to stay out of the way," Evie said.

"But that would defeat the purpose." Zelma looked at the others who both nodded. "We're hoping to tap into your expertise. Phillipa has been telling us about your recent experiences. We'll be counting on your input."

The trio made their way up the stairs, chatting excitedly.

Expertise?

"Are you gasping?" Phillipa whispered as the others moved out of hearing.

"Well... I am a little puzzled. Phillipa, what on earth did you say to them?"

"Only the truth. You mustn't be too modest. I think Detective Inspector O'Neill would be the first to admit you have been a valuable contributor to his investigations."

"I have only been an accidental participant." Evie wrung her hands together. "Toodles... I mean, my granny can't hear about any of it."

"I can see this might all become a dreadful inconvenience." Phillipa looked toward the stairs. "I think I will ask them to leave."

"Oh, no. No, you mustn't. I'm being silly. Everything will work out just fine." As they entered the drawing room, Evie heard the crunch of footsteps along the gravel path outside. Looking out of the French doors, she saw Tom. No doubt, he had come to assess the new guests and determine the security risk.

Evie smiled to herself and pictured the headlines. Society heiress held for ransom by a gang of scriptwriters.

"Tom's looking rather dapper today," Phillipa remarked. "He always dresses well, but there's something different today."

He came in through the French doors and greeted them with a wide smile.

"Savile Row?" Evie asked as she admired his gray suit and navy-blue tie. "What happened to your country squire tweed suits?"

Tom gave his cufflinks a twist. "Well, you know how your grandmother feels about men dressing appropriately. If she sees me in English country tweeds, I'll never hear the end of it."

"But that is appropriate…" Evie shook her head. "And she's not due to arrive for weeks."

"I'm playing it safe," Tom said, "and getting some practice in before she arrives."

Evie pressed her hand to her chest but couldn't contain her laughter. "You're scared of her. Oh, thank you. You've lightened my mood."

Tom bowed his head slightly and thickening his Boston accent, said, "I'm glad I could be of service, ma'am."

"Speaking of which…" She had almost forgotten about one of her most pressing concerns. Evie tapped her chin in thought. If she didn't act promptly, she might end up losing her butler. "I'd appreciate some fresh ideas." Evie lowered her voice. "I need to keep Edgar happy. He hasn't said anything yet, but I'm afraid he might be planning an exodus back to London. I wouldn't be surprised if he is scouting around and looking for another place of employment even as we speak."

"What do you have in mind?" Tom asked.

"I'm not really sure. All I know is that I wish him to feel this is the right place for him."

"So, you want him to feel more valued," Tom mused.

Casting a glance around the drawing room to make sure everything was as it should be, Evie said, "Please don't ask me how you can accomplish that. I'm afraid my imagination doesn't stretch that far."

"He could save your life," Phillipa suggested.

Tom and Evie both looked at her, their eyes wide with surprise and a hint of intrigue.

"I'm trying to engage my creativity." Phillipa sat on an armrest and swung her foot. "Let's see. Tom could hide somewhere out of sight and take a shot at you."

"Me?" Evie asked.

Phillipa waved her hand. "Of course, he'd miss you. You could make sure Edgar stood nearby to rescue you and when he does, you would feel so indebted to him, he'll never want to leave because he'll think your safety depends on him remaining in this house."

"That's rather extreme but…" Evie looked over her shoulder toward the door to make sure no one would overhear her, "I'm almost willing to try anything."

"Increase his income." Tom grinned. "That would work for me."

"Bribery and corruption is not beneath me. When I

found out he enjoys the theater, I gave him tickets and leave to go into town." And, she'd recently gifted him a handsome tiepin.

"You could play matchmaker," Phillipa suggested.

"What do you mean?"

"Well, he's not married. What if he were to fall in love with someone local? He'd have to stay here."

True. "Do we know someone suitable?" She gave it some thought. "I'm in favor of everyone living happily ever after, but I'm not sure I have the right experience to find him a perfect match."

Phillipa sunk into the chair. "With three other authors in the house, I think we might be able to come up with a plan for you."

A footman entered the drawing room and began setting up for morning tea.

Evie decided having the authors residing at Halton House just before her grandmother's visit might work in her favor. It seemed infinitely more satisfying to immerse herself in a world of make-believe than to have to deal with the reality of disappointing her granny in any way.

Sitting up, Phillipa mused, "You said he likes the theater… I could suggest writing a part for him in our play."

Evie brightened. "Oh, I think Edgar might rather enjoy that." Glancing over at Tom, she added, "It sounds far safer than having Tom shoot me."

"Do you think he might want to be the villain or the hero?" Phillipa asked.

Evie gave it some thought. She could picture Edgar as the hero but, secretly, she thought he might rather enjoy playing a villain…

Chapter Three

*All the world's a stage, and all the men
and women merely players
– William Shakespeare*

The library, Halton House

"So far, so good," Tom murmured as Evie showed her guests through to the library.

After morning refreshments, they had all taken a stroll around the estate, returning in time for lunch.

Conversation during lunch had been demure and restricted to pleasantries, mostly focusing on the theater and the authors' plans to write a play set in a country estate.

Since returning to England, Evie had entertained a few

guests for lunch and dinner while easing back into her life at Halton House, but the last couple of weeks had been relatively quiet. So much so, she felt slightly on edge. Her eyes wouldn't stop flitting about; her attention focused on her guests' comfort.

"Please feel free to use the library as your writing space," Evie offered. "Phillipa explained how it helps to have a place where you will not be interrupted."

Zelma Collins smiled. "That's very kind of you, Lady Woodridge, but we have recently adopted a new attitude. Since we can't always control our environment, we have decided to embrace all possibilities and have actually found ourselves thriving in the midst of chaos."

Evie had no idea what to say to that. Personally, she needed peace and quiet to work through her dilemmas...

"Evie will be only too happy to provide some chaos," Phillipa said, her tone cheerful.

"This is a splendid library," Ernestine Wilding commented.

"That's saying something," Phillipa gave Evie a bright smile. "Ernestine's father is quite a collector."

Ernestine Wilding shook her head. "He has devoted most of his life to reading yet he disapproves of my writing."

Evie wondered if he had reason to disapprove. She studied the tall, slender woman who could easily have graced the pages of the most popular fashion periodicals. Her fine features were highlighted by a slightly angular face and her pitch-black hair had been styled into a fashionable bob with a fringe hovering just a fraction above her delicately curved eyebrows.

Feeling somewhat self-conscious, Evie tugged at her

sleeve. Ernestine Wilding wore a bright orange blouse matched with a black and white houndstooth skirt and two-toned shoes, also in black and white. Evie felt downright provincial in her pleated sea green skirt and pretty pink blouse with spring blooms printed on it. Yes, she really needed to upgrade her wardrobe. Evie had no doubt it would be the first observation made by her grandmother.

"Phillipa mentioned you have a thespian working for you," Zelma said.

The petite brunette wore a black and beige striped low waisted dress with a long strand of pearls around her neck and the shortest bob Evie had ever seen on a woman.

Smiling, Evie said, "My butler does enjoy the theater."

Right on cue, Edgar entered the room and surprised Evie by once again making a formal announcement.

There had to be a message in there somewhere…

"The Most Honorable, the Dowager Countess of Woodridge."

"Thank you, Edgar." Henrietta strode in only to stop and ask, "Have you been heavy handed with your starch? Your posture seems to be stiffer than usual. Try to relax a little, Edgar."

"Yes, my lady."

When Edgar moved to exit the room, Zelma Collins said, "Oh, please don't leave."

Edgar looked confused.

Zelma Collins approached Edgar and engaged him in conversation. "The Countess tells us you are interested in the theater…"

Evie tried to listen in on the conversation, but Henrietta edged toward her and commandeered her attention.

"Evangeline. Would you mind telling me what I have walked into?"

Evie tried to formulate a response that would set Henrietta at ease, but before she could do so, Ernestine Wilding stepped forward.

"You mustn't mind Zelma, Lady Woodridge," Ernestine said. "She is rather fixated with her craft and sometimes forgets herself."

Evie made the introduction. "Henrietta, this is Ernestine Wilding. She is one of the writers I told you about."

"I see," Henrietta said with a sense of trepidation in her voice. "You are here to write a play."

"We hope so, yes."

"Where do you normally write your plays?" Henrietta asked.

Smiling, Ernestine said, "We all live in London. Both Zelma and Bernie have taken up residence in the West End and I live in Mayfair."

Mention of the prestigious address seemed to pacify the dowager who nevertheless gave Ernestine a head to toe sweep of her eyes.

"My grandfather is the Earl of Ansonfield and my father is Lord Wilding," Ernestine murmured.

Henrietta brightened. "Well, that makes you Lady Wilding."

"Yes, I suppose it does."

"Either you are Lady Wilding or you have been dispossessed of the privilege." Henrietta looked at Evie. "It's been known to happen when relatives disapprove."

Smiling, Ernestine said, "My grandfather dotes on me. He is more than happy to indulge my whims."

Henrietta's eyes twinkled. "And how do your parents feel about your whims?"

"My father is buried in his books so he rarely notices what I'm up to. In any case, he doesn't care much for plays. My mother reserves her opinions but I know she would much rather see me settled."

Henrietta nodded. "Mothers are required to worry about their children. Have you been presented?"

Evie glanced over at Edgar to see how he was faring with Zelma Collins. Smiling, she remembered her own presentation at court. So many of the young girls she had known at the time had vied for the honor of being presented. To Evie, it had been part of the whole rigmarole she had to undertake in order to fit in.

The whole process had been quite remarkable. Although, she had found it a little dull as most of the day had been spent waiting for her turn. Then again, she had only recently married and so her thoughts had been otherwise engaged. Since her husband had been an Earl, she had been expected to fulfill her duty by being presented to the monarch but Evie knew others had relied on their string-pulling abilities to secure an invitation.

"Evangeline looked resplendent in her gown," Henrietta reminisced as she continued to engage Ernestine in conversation.

Evie didn't comment. Personally, she had found the gown odd. White, low-necked and short-sleeved, she'd had to contend with a train four yards long and three yards wide. The long white gloves, white veil, and three white feathers in her hair had been *de rigueur*.

All that trouble just to make a deep curtsy to each royal in attendance. Remembering the details, Evie laughed to herself. Advancing toward the dais where the royals had been seated, her train had swept along behind her. After her curtsey, an attendant had then handed her the train, saying, 'Your train, Madam." As if she could have forgotten she had been dragging it along. She had then been instructed to throw the train over her arm and depart.

Had it been a life changing experience? Hardly. Nevertheless, she had appreciated the process as well as the resplendent setting.

Henrietta turned to one of the scriptwriters, Bernie Peters, but the young woman had already surrounded herself with a pile of books from the shelves. Finding another target, she signaled toward Zelma Collins, and said, "Your guest seems to be intrigued by Edgar."

"I believe she is trying to entice him into participating in their play. Although, I'm not sure what she means to do with him." Evie watched Edgar nodding. So far, he hadn't made any attempt to cut the conversation short. Which could mean anything, Evie thought. She trusted Edgar to be polite, but Evie knew he could be reserved and employ the tactic to escape an uncomfortable situation. To her surprise, he seemed to be intrigued.

"My lady." Ernestine looked at Evie who promptly invited her to again address her by her name. "Evie. I wonder if you might be interested in assisting us. We discussed this during our drive here. As soon as we have the first scene written, we would like to stage a rehearsal."

Evie assured her, "As I said, you're welcome to use the library. Is there anything else you might need? Perhaps some props?"

"Yes, an actress. How would you feel about playing one of the roles?"

Ernestine Wilding's invitation to participate in her play kept Evie's mind occupied for the rest of the evening and well into the night.

At least, it served the purpose of keeping her thoughts away from worrying about her granny's surprise visit, or the possibility of losing her butler.

Sitting back, she once again fixated on the problem. Good butlers were hard to come by. She would do just about anything to keep Edgar happy…

"Caro, you'd tell me if you heard any whispers about Edgar wanting to leave, wouldn't you?" Evie asked as she prepared for bed.

"Of course, milady. I wouldn't dream of keeping anything from you."

Evie finished removing the gloves she had worn for dinner and happened to glance up in time to catch Caro's expression reflected in the mirror. "Did you just wince?"

"Me? Wince? Why would I do that, milady?"

"I don't know. You tell me. Are you unhappy about something?" Evie watched Caro clearly struggling with her conscience. Evie considered encouraging her to reveal her concerns but Caro must have felt strongly enough to not need any further persuasion.

"Well, if you must know, Edgar told quite an elaborate tale this evening about being invited to participate in a play."

To Evie, that sounded like good news. If Edgar had shared the information with the downstairs servants, that could only mean he had embraced the idea. "Do you disapprove?" Evie asked.

Caro's eyebrows drew downward. "Oh, so it is true."

"Well... Yes. Did you think Edgar had been fibbing?"

Caro shrugged. "He can be a little uppity sometimes. In fact, whenever he goes into town to see one of his plays, he becomes quite unbearable, putting on airs and talking as if he were on the stage putting on a performance."

Evie turned slightly and smiled at Caro. "But that sounds like fun. Is he any good?"

Caro rolled her eyes. "Mrs. Horace seems to think so. She finds it all very amusing."

Evie clapped her hands. If the cook found him amusing, then he must have some talent, perhaps even a hidden talent, she thought. "This could work out really well."

Caro pursed her lips.

"Caro, I get the feeling you disapprove."

Caro looked away and murmured, "He's not the only one with talent."

"Oh, is there someone else?" Belatedly, Evie recalled how much Caro had enjoyed playing the role of her distant relative recently, Lady Carolina Thwaites. "Would you like me to ask if..."

Caro beamed. "Oh, yes. Would you? Oh, that would be marvelous."

"Consider it done."

As Caro turned her attention to tidying up, she said, "Would you mind if I wear my new dress? That is... When I read my lines. I think it would be easier for me to step into character if I wear my Sunday best."

"Yes, of course." Evie turned her attention to removing her earrings. "Here's an idea. Why don't we go into the village tomorrow and visit the dressmaker? You can have something new. My treat. She has been working on some new gowns for me and I had intended going in for a fitting next week, but I think I need to organize some more gowns. I doubt I'll have time to go into town and, unless I do something about my clothes, my grandmother is bound to notice I'm not keeping up with the times. I hear Mrs. Green has hired a new assistant who's worked in Paris. I'm hoping I'll be able to fool my granny. Well? What do you think?"

Caro gave her a worried look. "Oh, yes… It sounds like a perfect plan."

"Caro. I've known you long enough to recognize the signs. I thought you'd be happy. Is there something you're not telling me?"

"Well… I thought you might want to avoid going into the village. At least for the time being."

Evie stilled. She had enjoyed an entire evening without giving a single thought to Mrs. Sheffield, now the name jumped out at her. She would hate to hear her name mentioned, especially in connection to herself. She couldn't think of any other reason why Caro would think she'd want to avoid going into the village.

"I'm not sure I understand what you mean," Evie said.

"Well, I don't have all the details because I'd been listening to Edgar prattling on about the play, but I also caught snippets of another conversation. Mrs. Arnold went into the village today. She overheard a conversation and it had something to do with a woman remarking on your accent."

"My accent?"

"Your lack of a proper British accent, to be precise, something she found highly inappropriate because… because of your title. You know how Mrs. Arnold disapproves of spreading gossip. Well, she made an exception because she felt the woman had overstepped her mark."

"And?"

"As I said, I don't have all the details, but she did mention something about an altercation."

Evie gasped. "With whom?"

Caro looked up and tapped her chin. "Let me think. Oh, yes. Mrs. Sheffield."

Impossible, Evie thought. "What exactly did she have to say about my accent?"

Caro stepped away. "I'm ever so sorry I mentioned it. My mother always says I have the worst timing and she's always told me never to break bad news in the evening because it could be disruptive to a person's sleep." Caro sighed. "I really should listen to her."

"Caro. What did Mrs. Sheffield say?"

"Promise you won't get cross. She… She finds the way you express yourself and your accent offensive."

"M-my… my accent? And what is wrong with the way I express myself? It's not as if I sound like Ward McAllister." Evie cupped her chin in her hand and shook her head in disbelief.

"Ward McAllister? Who is he?"

Evie waved her other hand. "Oh, he's someone my granny met once at a picnic in Newport many, many years ago. The man used to throw lavish picnics and never pay for anything. He'd say something along the lines of 'Eg Winthrop will send a saddle of lamb, don' cha know, don' cha see. Mrs. Astor's chef will garnish a salmon, don' cha know, don' cha see.' My granny does a better impersonation."

"I'm sorry," Caro offered. "I've upset you."

"Oh, don't worry about it. I've been upset for a couple of days now. For heaven's sake, I invited the woman into my home. You would think she'd have better manners. I don't believe I have ever heard anyone being so critical." Evie huffed out a breath.

"I suppose I shouldn't mention what she said about the food…"

Evie gasped. "No. Please tell me she didn't criticize the food."

Caro gave a small nod.

"But everyone always enjoys the food offered at Halton House." Evie surged to her feet. "What I find most distressing is the fact the others enjoyed the afternoon tea. Mrs. Sheffield is not only criticizing me, she is also belittling everyone else who enjoys what I have to offer." She gave a firm nod. "The dowager is right. I need to put a stop to her. The sooner, the better."

Chapter Four

*A thing long expected takes the form of the
unexpected when at last it comes*
– Mark Twain

The Village of Halton

"It's a lovely spring day for a walk, but time is of the essence." Evie felt guilty abandoning her guests even though she knew they didn't need her hovering around. Nevertheless, she wanted to return to Halton House as soon as possible and continue working on the menus for her granny's visit. "Thank you for driving us, Tom."

"My pleasure."

Evie tipped her head back and smiled up at the sky.

Another perfect day in the countryside, she thought. Far too pleasant to risk running into Mrs. Sheffield.

Evie's smile faded. Her back teeth gritted with determination. She refused to allow the woman to take possession of her thoughts.

Leaning over the passenger seat, Evie smiled at Caro. Seated on the rumble seat, her maid had one hand on her hat and the other on the backrest, her knuckles showing white.

"I almost forgot to tell you," Evie said. "I telephoned the town house and spoke with Millicent. She will arrive either later today or early tomorrow morning. You might want to let the downstairs staff know. She will call from the train station. In case I forget, please let Edmonds know. He'll need to collect her at the train station."

Tom turned into the main street, driving at a sedate pace. The villagers were out and about tending to their daily business and stopping for chats. Evie smiled with appreciation. She could live anywhere in the world, and yet, she couldn't imagine moving away any time soon. Yes, she lived up at the big house, but everyone had accepted her as part of the small community. This was home.

"Oh," Caro exclaimed right before her arm appeared between Tom and Evie, her finger stretched out and pointed at something ahead.

Evie looked up and gasped.

"What do you think that is all about?" Caro asked, her finger still pointed toward their destination, Mrs. Green's dressmaking shop.

"I daresay, we will soon find out," Tom murmured and stopped the motor car across the green. "By the way, next time you notice something unusual, please ease into it. My heart is punching hard against my chest."

Two police constables stood by the front door blocking the entrance to Mrs. Green's establishment. A few local villagers had gathered there, standing a few feet away, almost as if they had been herded away from the front door and told to keep their distance.

"Do you think someone has broken in?" Caro asked.

"What made you say that?"

"We've never had a burglary in the village," Caro explained. "If given the choice, I would prefer a burglary over a murder."

Evie exchanged a look with Tom that spoke of amusement and asked, "Have you developed an aversion to murder?"

"I haven't given it any thought, milady. I suppose I only wished to avoid sounding ghoulish."

Tom emerged from the motor car and helped Caro climb down from the rumble seat. Evie didn't wait for him to open the passenger door. She emerged from the motor car and stood for a moment in front of a store window studying the reflection of Mrs. Green's store across the street.

"Someone is bound to know something," Caro suggested. "Would you like me to ask? I'll be discreet."

"I suppose we should all go." Everyone who'd been standing by had now turned to look at them.

"Oh," Caro yelped. "We seem to have attracted their attention. Should we look away and pretend we haven't noticed them noticing us?"

"I don't see why we should." Tom shrugged. "We have as much right to stand here gawking as they have."

Yes, but Evie would bet anything the people standing across the street knew a lot more than they did. However, she couldn't send Caro to scout for information because everyone would recognize her as Evie's maid. The Countess of Woodridge simply couldn't appear to be taking part in anything that resembled a scandal. She had no trouble hearing Henrietta say it would be beneath her.

"Perhaps we should wait and see what happens," Evie suggested. "Let's go into the tearoom and sit by the window to watch the proceedings."

"Wait," Caro said. "Someone is coming out. Oh... Oh. *Oh, my goodness*."

If Evie had not seen it with her own eyes, she would not have believed it.

Henrietta appeared at Mrs. Green's door, her parasol in hand. She stopped for a moment to take in the scene. Then, lifting her chin, she walked to her motor car. Her chauffeur hurried to hold the door open for her. As the car pulled away, Henrietta looked out of the passenger window and straight at Evie.

"I suppose this means our tea will have to wait," Evie said. "At least until we reach the dower house."

They all piled back into the roadster and followed Henrietta's car at a discreet distance.

Once they reached the dower house, they made their way to the front door. Just as Tom lifted his hand to knock on the front door, they heard the distant sound of a siren.

"An ambulance," Caro murmured.

"We shouldn't jump to conclusions," Evie warned.

Hearing the door open, they all turned and saw Henrietta's butler, Bradley, looking down at them.

"Good morning, Bradley. Is the dowager receiving

visitors this morning?" Evie asked even as she took a step forward.

"Certainly, my lady." He opened the door wider and gestured them through.

"That's a relief," Caro murmured. "I feared the dowager might have been in too much shock to see anyone."

"Why would you think that?" Evie asked. Although, she too had entertained a similar thought.

"Something has clearly happened. Should I wait out in the hallway?" Caro asked.

"No, I'm sure Henrietta won't mind if you come into the drawing room."

They found the dowager standing by the window.

When they entered, she turned and rushed toward Evie.

"My dear Evangeline. You have spared me a trip to Halton House. I would have rushed there straightaway but I needed to compose myself. Do sit down. Bradley will bring in some tea. I have had the most horrendous morning. You would not believe it even if you had been there to witness it. The police questioned me." Henrietta pressed a lace handkerchief to her brow. "I have been held as a suspect. The news will have traveled the length and breadth of the entire county by now. I shall henceforth be known as the notorious dowager."

"Henrietta. What happened?"

"I stand accused of assault."

Chapter Five

The dowager… Accused of assault?

It took two cups of tea and a splash of brandy before Henrietta finally explained how she had visited Mrs. Green's store that morning. Although, the brandy caused her to meander her way through her tale.

Giving a brisk smile, Henrietta said, "Mrs. Green has a new dressmaker, Abigail. Lovely girl."

Evie exchanged a look with Tom and Caro who had both stood back giving Evie ample room to deal with the situation.

Henrietta continued, "As you know, Mrs. Green has a drawing room set up in the rear of her shop for her more distinguished patrons."

Doing her best to remain calm, Evie nodded. "Yes, I've often admired the dainty pieces she has on display."

Henrietta shrugged. "Her tea service is somewhat dated but one can always appreciate good quality china."

Evie clasped the dowager's hand. "Henrietta, what happened?"

"Well, I had been sitting in the pretty drawing room, admiring a picture when I heard the most dreadful remarks coming from the front of the store where Mrs. Green has an area designated for the general public. I'll spare you the details of my reaction. Suffice to say, I went through several stages in quick succession. From disbelief to utter astonishment to extreme displeasure. This resulted in me having words with that dreadful woman, Mrs. Sheffield." Henrietta pressed her hand to her chest.

Evie made an attempt to picture the scene but failed miserably. "I… I don't understand."

"Which part don't you understand, my dear?"

Evie looked confused enough for the dowager to comprehend her meaning.

Drawing in a calming breath, the dowager recounted her experience. "As I waited for the seamstress to make a few adjustments to my gown, I overheard Mrs. Sheffield speaking ill of you. I could not stand by and allow that dreadful woman to drag your name through the mud. So, I made my way to the front of the store and confronted her. She did not look surprised to see me. I can only assume she meant for me to overhear her remarks."

Goodness, Evie thought. What could she possibly have said?

"It really does not bear repeating, my dear," Henrietta said almost as if she had read Evie's thoughts. "Needless to say, she deserved a thorough dressing down and that could only come from me. I feel partly responsible for allowing her behavior to continue unchecked for as long as it has. Although, in reality, it has only been a few days since she has launched her attack but the woman's spiteful words have the power to spread like wildfire and influence other people." Henrietta gave an impatient shake of her head. "I shall never understand why people are so driven by negativity and the need to make their mark in the world with it."

Evie's brow puckered. Exactly how long had Mrs. Sheffield been waging this war against her?

The dowager continued, "I took the liberty to inform her she would no longer be received at Halton House."

Evie heard Caro gasp.

"You were within your rights, Henrietta. I'm sorry she upset you so." Her eyebrows drew downward. "We saw two constables standing outside. Who called them in?"

Henrietta shifted. "Mrs. Sheffield went on a rampage right before she swooned and collapsed. No one knew what to do. Mrs. Green, thank goodness, acted promptly and called... Well, she called someone. Either the police or the doctor." Henrietta leaned back. "What will your grandmother think of me now?"

"Don't you worry about my granny," Evie assured her. "She would never think less of you, especially not since you were doing your duty." Glancing over her shoulder, she made eye contact with Tom. She nudged her head in the general direction of the village and hoped he would understand her meaning. The sooner they had some hard facts, the better.

Giving a nod, he stepped out.

"Is there something I can do?" Caro asked.

"Oh yes, my dear. Could you fetch my shawl, please?

It's Mariah's day off." The dowager turned to Evie. "That's my new maid. Did I tell you I had a new maid?"

Evie patted her hand. "I think I should send for Dr. Browning."

"Oh, you needn't bother. I'm only feeling slightly shaken by the ordeal. More tea. Yes, that's what I need." Henrietta stared into space, her lips slightly parted, her eyes not blinking. Snapping out of her stupor, she pulled on her lace handkerchief and then turned her attention to a pretty brooch. She straightened it and then looked at her hands…

Evie felt helpless. She'd never seen Henrietta fretting.

A moment later, Caro appeared at the door and signaled to Evie.

"I'll be back shortly." Evie stepped out into the hallway and whispered, "I've never seen the dowager in such a state." She placed a call to Dr. Browning. His assistant took a message and promised the doctor would attend to the dowager as soon as he could. Ending the call, Evie turned to Caro and saw the look of concern on her face. "What is it, Caro?"

"News has reached the downstairs servants, milady," Caro said. "No one would say how they heard it but I'm guessing Mrs. Sheffield's maid has something to do with it. Apparently, the dowager assaulted Mrs. Sheffield with her parasol."

Evie pressed her hand to her mouth. It seemed so out of character for Henrietta. "I… I can't believe it. In fact, I can't even picture it."

"Perhaps it's only a rumor," Caro suggested.

"Oh, yes. Let's hope it is. I wish Tom would hurry up

with some news. I really don't wish to push Henrietta for more information."

"With your permission, I would like to return to the village and see what I can find out."

Evie nodded. "Yes. Yes, that would be good. Thank you, Caro." She took the shawl and returned to the drawing room where she found Henrietta laughing softly.

"I'm sorry," Henrietta said. "I realize it must look odd to find me laughing but I'm only now remembering how Mrs. Sheffield sputtered. I doubt anyone has ever dared to stand up to her. I found the experience most gratifying even if the aftermath has left me feeling somewhat unsettled. I'm not accustomed to raising my voice but she left me no choice."

Evie arranged the shawl around Henrietta's shoulders and settled on a chair by her side. "Please don't be annoyed with me. I have telephoned Dr. Browning."

Henrietta's eyes brightened. "Now I'm remembering Mrs. Green's look of shock. I always found her to be somewhat timid. Yet, she managed to find her voice. She accused us of lacking good manners, refinement and grace. Unfortunately, she stepped in the way of Mrs. Sheffield's tantrum and received a fist in the face." Henrietta's voice lowered to an apologetic whisper, "I'm afraid we may need to find another dressmaker."

Chapter Six

When a bad situation turns worse…

When Tom and Caro returned to the dower house, they both related similar stories. Henrietta had not exaggerated and word about her confrontation had spread throughout the village. However, Henrietta would be pleased to learn she had been hailed as a heroine and praised for her steadfast retaliation.

"Perhaps I should withhold that tidbit." Evie wrung her hands together. "It will only go to her head. Then again, I don't wish her to feel she will never be able to set foot outside her house again." Evie looked toward the drawing room door. "Dr. Browning is with her now." Turning back, she saw Tom and Caro having a wordless conversation. "Is there something else?"

Caro nudged Tom. "You go first. If you leave anything out, I'll fill in the gaps."

"Do I need to sit down for this?" Evie asked.

"Perhaps it might be best if you do." Caro drew out a chair for her. Evie's legs wobbled slightly as she eased down onto it.

Tom cleared his throat. "Do you remember hearing the ambulance siren?"

"How could I forget? Actually... Yes, I had forgotten. What about it? Did Mrs. Sheffield take a turn for the worst? Henrietta mentioned something about Mrs. Green coming between them and Mrs. Sheffield landing a blow on her face. I will have to dig deep for some sympathy for Mrs. Sheffield. I suppose she must have suffered some distress too. Or is it Mrs. Green? Is something wrong with her?" Evie stopped and drew in a shaky breath. Belatedly, she realized she'd blabbered on because she didn't want to hear the rest of the news. Evie gave a small nod. "I'm sorry, you were saying..."

"There's no easy way to say this." Tom looked down at the floor and then back up at Evie. "The ambulance took away a body."

Startled by the news, Evie pressed her hand to her chest. "Mrs. Green?"

Tom gave a slow shake of his head. When he spoke, his voice carried the caution of someone who knew he was about to deliver bad news, "Mrs. Sheffield."

Evie's head moved from side to side as she slipped into a state of instant denial. Oh, no. No. No. This couldn't be happening. Someone had made a mistake.

Determined to confirm it, Caro gave a vigorous nod. "She's dead. Stone cold dead. Gone to meet her maker dead."

The door to the drawing room opened and Dr. Browning stepped out.

Setting aside her shock, Evie asked, "How is the dowager?"

"As well as can be expected," he said. "She sounds cohesive but still shaken by her ordeal. I have recommended resting for a few days. Yes, peace and quiet. That's what she needs."

Evie's fingers wrapped around the armrest. "Dr. Browning, did you... did you by any chance attend to Mrs. Sheffield?"

Checking his watch, he gave a distracted nod. "Yes, I did."

While she sensed he wouldn't divulge more than he could, Evie pressed him for more information. "Did you arrive in time?"

"No, I'm afraid not. I'm sorry, Lady Woodridge. That is all I am permitted to say."

"Does that mean you are under police instructions?" she asked.

"That is correct."

Pending an investigation, Evie assumed.

"Please try to avoid upsetting the dowager. This is not the sort of news she should hear just yet," he said.

Bradley appeared and handed Dr. Browning his hat.

"Not a word of this to the dowager," Evie said when the doctor left.

"Begging your pardon, milady," Caro said, "but she's bound to ask and her staff will have all the details by now. Or, at least, some sort of version of the events."

Evie turned to the butler. "Bradley."

"Yes, my lady."

"Please have a word with the downstairs staff. Everyone must tread with caution and refrain from mentioning anything about this unfortunate incident. The dowager is bound to ask for news, but you must do your utmost to distract her. Can I trust you to be discreet?"

"Certainly, my lady."

She turned to enter the drawing room, but a knock at the front door had Evie swinging around. They all held their breaths as Bradley attended to the door.

Standing at a distance, they were all at a disadvantage, unable to hear or see who it was. A moment later, however, Bradley closed the door.

"The mailman, my lady. I believe he wished to get some information but I persuaded him to move on."

He set the letters on a silver tray and carried them into the drawing room. Evie, Tom and Caro followed and settled around the dowager who now sat by the window.

"Thank you, Bradley. You can leave the letters on my desk. I shall attend to my correspondence later in the day when my mind has cleared." Turning to Evie, she said, "Heavens, in my youth, I often heard my grandmama recommending the waters at Bath. Even though I knew the healing and calming properties of warm mineral springs assisted in one's wellbeing, I never quite understood what she meant. Now… I think I should take myself to Bath for a few days."

Evie didn't like the idea of the dowager traveling by herself or being alone. "Perhaps you can postpone that for the time being. I shall instruct Bradley to pack some clothes. I want you to come to Halton House with us. I cannot, in good conscious, allow you to remain here alone." Evie looked around. "By the way, where is Sara?"

Henrietta waved her hand. "Oh, she's in town visiting with friends."

Sara, Lady Woodridge, Evie's mother-in-law, would need to be informed. Evie added the task to her list and said, "Then it's settled. You are coming with me."

"Oh, dear. I would hate to be a burden."

"Nonsense. You need to distract yourself and I... I need your help with the menus. I'm afraid I have made quite a muddle of it all. As it is, my granny will probably think I'm not even fit to run a honky-tonk."

The dowager raised her eyebrows. "Honky-what?"

Evie dug around her mind. "I think you know them as coaching inns."

"Oh... I see." Looking somewhat puzzled, the dowager added, "Is it just me or does that sound rather disreputable? My dear, is there something you are not telling me?"

As far as distractions went, it served its purpose.

Chapter Seven

Evie left Caro in charge of organizing the dowager's luggage and accompanying her back to the house. Meanwhile, she returned to Halton House with Tom. They only had a short distance to cover, yet the fact they remained silent appeared to make the journey longer.

When they passed the gatehouse, Evie made a conscious effort to focus on admiring the surrounding countryside with its rolling hills and majestic trees. Heavenly spring sunshine, she thought.

"I can smell it in the air. Freshly laundered linen," Evie murmured.

"Pardon?" Tom asked.

Evie closed her eyes, drew in a deep breath, and tried to hold on to the feeling of quiet, simple enjoyment. "Oh, nothing." She watched the house come into view. It looked resplendent in the sunshine, the windows sparkling as if calling out a cheerful greeting.

Holding the passenger door open for her, Tom said, "I'll meet you inside shortly. I need to stretch my legs."

"Yes, I don't blame you. I wish I could join you, but I need to pave the way and prepare the others."

Hurrying up the few steps leading up to the portico entrance, Evie was too distracted by her thoughts to take notice of the footman who opened the door for her. When she did notice, it struck her as odd. Edgar rarely allowed anyone else to take charge of the task, but being preoccupied with the morning's events, Evie decided not to ask for explanations.

Removing her gloves, she glanced up in time to see Phillipa rushing toward her. "Oh, good. You've saved me the trouble of hunting you down."

"Yes, I've been keeping an eye out for you," Phillipa said. "I wanted to talk to you before you went into the library."

Evie told herself to remain calm. Yet, she couldn't help exclaiming, "Heavens! Has something happened?"

"Oh, no... not really. Only, remember how Zelma Collins asked Edgar to play a role..."

Evie gave a tentative nod. "Has he changed his mind?" She really couldn't deal with another problem now or put any more energy into pacifying Edgar.

"On the contrary. Zelma wanted to try something new. She has finished the first scene and now she wishes to try some unrehearsed lines."

"Ad libbing?" Evie said, her thoughts miles away.

"Yes, and Zelma needs everyone to simply go with the flow. She believes she might gain some inspiration from the exercise."

Evie finished removing her gloves and told herself to

focus on the here and now. "Are you about to tell me Edgar is currently in the library ad libbing?"

"As a matter of fact, yes. And he's rather good at it."

Evie handed her gloves and coat to a footman and followed Phillipa into the library. With everyone gathered in the one room, she would only have to make the announcement about the morning's events once.

"Ah, Ms. Evie Parker. What news do you bring from the village?" Edgar asked.

Evie stopped in her tracks. A swift survey of the library placed the three scriptwriters all sitting by the fireplace. Edgar stood in front of them, a hand on the mantle and his other hand hitched on his coat pocket.

Phillipa leaned in and whispered, "I suppose I should have warned you about that. Edgar is Lord Edgar and you are…"

Evie gave her a brisk smile. "Yes, I think I know who I am." Plain Evie Parker, she thought.

"I hope you won't mind too much. Zelma thinks we would all deliver some intriguing insights if we reversed roles or changed them slightly."

Evie took a deep swallow. "So, who are you playing?"

Phillipa gave her a wide smile. "I'm Lady Phillipa and I'm playing the part of the relative no one talks about."

"M-my relative?"

"Yes, there have been several attempts to lock me up in an asylum but I seem to hold some sort of power over the family. We haven't quite figured out what. Since everyone ignores me, I tend to see and hear more than anyone, which means I know everyone's secrets. Or, at least, I hope I do."

Evie turned toward Edgar. He remained in character for a second and then shifted.

Seeing him about to offer an apology, Evie said, "Lord Edgar. Thank you for inviting me."

"Thank you," Phillipa mouthed. "And... you actually live here as his poor relation."

"Oh... I see. My apologies." Evie floundered. "So... Do I just say the first thing that comes to mind?"

"Yes. That's the idea."

Evie sifted through everything that had happened and tried to figure out the best way to share the news about Mrs. Sheffield but her mind blanked when Zelma Collins rushed toward her.

"Lady Woodridge. Thank you for going along with our little game. I hope it doesn't inconvenience you."

"Well... I must say, it's not the best timing. However..." Her shoulders lowered. "I suppose we could all do with the distraction."

Zelma smiled. "I'm so happy to hear you say so, my lady."

Evie remembered she had given Zelma leave to call her by her first name. Or had she? So much had happened since her guests' arrival and even before then...

Zelma continued, "Would we be imposing too much if we carried on throughout the day? We realize Edgar has duties to perform, but it would be ever so helpful if we could gather here for a couple of hours this afternoon and see what we can come up with."

"Yes, of course." Evie had no idea what took possession of her when she said, "You might want to work out a schedule which will suit Edgar." It seemed reasonable to bar all restrictions. After all, she had opened the doors to her home in goodwill. Excusing herself, she strode out.

Heavens, what had she just walked into? Evie took a moment to gather her thoughts only to realize she had failed to share the news about Mrs. Sheffield and, most importantly, Henrietta's involvement.

Evie considered returning to the library, but then she looked up and saw that Henrietta and Caro had arrived and they were making a beeline for her.

"There you are, Evangeline," Henrietta said. "I told your maid I wished to spend a few moments in the library. I think a good book is what I need to take my mind off this morning's distressing events."

Evie looked over her shoulder. She couldn't let Henrietta walk in on that scene. Who knew how she would react… "Oh, but I'd hoped you would help me with the menus."

"If you insist. I don't wish to burden you with my company. You know I'm quite capable of entertaining myself."

"Nonsense. You'll be doing me a great favor by helping me." Evie guided Henrietta away from the library. "Let's go into the morning drawing room. Oh, Caro… I left my notes in the library. Would you mind fetching them for me, please?" She couldn't think of any other way to direct Caro to go into the library without alerting Henrietta.

Despite everything that had happened, Evie knew it would be best to continue on with the plans they had set into motion. The sooner Caro knew what the others were doing, the better. Her maid had already missed out on getting a new dress, Evie didn't want her to also miss out on participating in the play. As for Henrietta…

She would have to find a way to let her know what the scriptwriters were up to and hope Henrietta didn't disapprove. Although, Evie couldn't think of a reason why she would.

"I'll ring for some tea," Evie said as they entered the drawing room.

Henrietta walked toward the middle of the sun-filled room and looked around her.

"Is something wrong?" Evie asked.

The dowager made a gesture with her hand as if to diminish the significance of the thought she'd been entertaining. "Well, if you must know, being questioned by the police made me realize my days enjoying freedom might be numbered. In fact, I shall probably end my days in a dark prison cell."

Evie laughed. "Oh, Henrietta. How could you possibly think that?"

Henrietta lowered her voice. "You should have seen the way the constable looked at me. At first, I thought he might have been indulging me as if I had been relating a fanciful tale. Gradually, however, he seemed to become more serious. When he drew out his notebook, I knew he meant business."

"Where was Mrs. Sheffield while this was happening?" Had she already died? No, of course not. Evie ran through the sequence of events and realized the doctor must have arrived soon after Henrietta had left Mrs. Green's establishment. That meant Mrs. Sheffield had died within those few minutes. Or at least, by the time they had reached the dower house when they had heard the ambulance siren…

"Let me think." Henrietta looked up and brushed a finger across her chin. "Oh, yes. She'd collapsed onto a chair... quite unceremoniously. In fact, I remember her moaning. Mrs. Green rushed to her side and fanned her."

"If you must know," Evie said, "I'm having trouble believing any of this."

"Oh, but it's all too true. When I saw her raise her parasol..."

Evie's eyes widened with shock. "Pardon?"

"Oh, yes. She meant to attack me, I'm sure."

"What did you do?"

"I parried her attack with a countermove."

"You did what? But... How?"

"I raised my own parasol and intercepted her blow." Henrietta gave her a small smile. "My fencing instructor would have been proud of me. It has been many years since I held a foil..." She made a thrusting gesture with an imaginary sword. "But I remembered enough."

"And?"

Henrietta's eyes brightened and she lifted her chin. "I disarmed her, of course. Yes, indeed, Monsieur Bouchard would have been proud."

"Dare I ask what happened next?"

"She cried out and, moments later, she collapsed onto the chair as if her legs had buckled from right under her. I believe she succumbed to the element of surprise. I must say, I feel rather annoyed with the constable. He appeared to think I had made it all up but Mrs. Green confirmed it all. Only then did he believe me. I'm almost inclined to take exception to his lack of trust."

Evie gestured to the chairs near the window. At some point, she would have to tell Henrietta about Mrs.

Sheffield dying. Looking out of the window, she wondered if Tom had deliberately chosen to make himself scarce in order to avoid the inevitable scene.

Henrietta, bless her soul, offered a change of subject. "How are your writers getting on?"

Evie debated whether or not to tell Henrietta about the interesting and unexpected development. In the end, she decided in favor of it, thinking it would work well as a distraction for the dowager. If she chose to disapprove, so much the better. It would take the focus away from her confrontation with Mrs. Sheffield and give her something else to think about.

"I'm glad you brought it up." As Evie spoke, she could see Henrietta doing her best to pay attention, but Evie couldn't be fooled. The dowager's focus remained elsewhere, making it inadvisable to share the rest of the news with her.

Chapter Eight

"Chaos often breeds life, when order breeds habit." – Henry Adams

Tom returned a few minutes before the lunch gong rang.

When Henrietta heard it, she sighed. "I hope your guests won't think me rude. I am going to retire for a rest. I'm not feeling particularly hungry. Please make my excuses."

When the dowager left, Tom murmured, "You still haven't told her."

Evie shook her head.

"She'll need to know eventually."

"Are you offering to tell her?" Evie asked and wished she could delegate the task of breaking the news to the dowager.

"I think it would be best coming from you."

"In that case, I don't see the point of mentioning it until the police decide how Mrs. Sheffield died, if indeed they are even looking into the death. I imagine Mrs. Sheffield had some sort of pre-existing condition no one knew about and that brought about her demise. If I tell Henrietta now, she might think she was somehow responsible."

"You're really concerned about the dowager."

"Of course, I am. I've never seen her looking so frail."

Tom's eyebrows rose slightly.

"Well, she didn't look frail when she told me how she fended off Mrs. Sheffield's attack, but earlier, she appeared to be in a state of shock." It hadn't really surprised Evie. Women like Henrietta were not accustomed to verbal confrontations, in fact, Evie struggled to remember if she'd ever heard the dowager raising her voice or even arguing.

"Fended off an attack?" Intrigued, Tom invited her to share the tale, which she did as they made their way to the dining room.

Normally, she would have attended to her guests, making sure everyone found their way, but she trusted Phillipa would take good care of them, and she had. When they entered the dining room, the others were all finding their places at the table.

"Ah, Evie Parker, what news do you bring from the village?" Edgar said as she made her way toward her place at the table. Her butler had his back to her, so he hadn't actually seen her entering the dining room.

"Heavens," Evie murmured under her breath, Edgar had taken his ad libbing to heart. Taking her seat, she said, "Lord Edgar, I have some troubling news."

Startled, Edgar swung around. His surprised expression

suggested he had been practicing his lines and confirmed Evie's suspicion he hadn't expected her to walk in at that precise moment.

"My apologies, my lady. I did not see you enter."

"Do carry on, Edgar," she encouraged.

Bowing his head slightly, he continued his task of overseeing the footmen.

She gave the others an acknowledging nod. Zelma Collins sat directly opposite Evie with Bernie and Ernestine sitting at either side of her. While Phillipa took her place next to Evie.

"My lady," Zelma Collins said, "your butler has displayed exceptional thespian skills. Not only has he provided a unique perspective for his character but he has also succeeded in reinvigorating our play, taking it to a new level."

"I'm very pleased to hear you say so." Evie caught Edgar's small smile and decided to throw caution and propriety to the wind. "Edgar, please feel free to continue participating. I'm sure the footmen will be only too happy to step in and help you out. In fact, I think you should join us for lunch."

"Lunch, my lady?"

"Yes. Pull up a chair. If I am going to participate, I need to be fully conversant with all the characters."

"Pull… up…a…"

"Oh, do sit down, Edgar." Evie wanted to say she would do anything to ensure he stayed on as butler. She knew her suggestion broke all protocols. The household staff preferred everyone to know their place, and any breach was bound to be viewed as disruptive. But there were exceptions.

Throughout the years, Evie had attended countless ghillies balls where neighbors, estate workers and household servants mingled with the gentry without any difficulties. "Just this once, I'm sure it won't kill us to have the butler, otherwise known as Lord Edgar, sitting with us for lunch."

"As you wish, my lady."

Watching him hesitate, Evie refrained from rolling her eyes. She couldn't put her finger on the feeling taking a hold of her. Needless to say, it all felt strangely unfamiliar, almost as if she'd reached a crossroad and she had no idea which direction to take. She only knew she needed to keep moving. "It's Evie Parker."

Phillipa whispered, "You are a champion. Will I be required to repay your generosity?"

"I'll have to think about it," Evie whispered in jest. Glancing up, Evie thought she heard Edgar murmur something about this being highly unconventional and irregular.

Instead of letting the remark go, Evie said, "I'm sure our guests are quite accustomed to unusual circumstances, *Lord Edgar*."

They all nodded.

Settling back, Evie took a moment to appreciate the intricate folds in the table napkin and smiled as she recalled Henrietta once saying that while she arranged a serviette on her lap, Evie arranged a table napkin. She'd never had any issues with her American way of doing things... In fact, the dowager had always stressed the fact she would not expect Evie to change her ways since one could remain the same and still embrace new customs.

Evie tilted her head in thought. Even after all these

years, she sometimes still struggled to understand the dowager's meaning...

Arranging the table napkin on her lap, Evie laughed under her breath.

"Are you all right?" Tom asked.

She gave him a small nod. "I think I'm reacting to Henrietta's shock by losing myself in introspection."

"Introspection? What are you thinking about?" he asked.

"Table napkins and serviettes."

He laughed. "What would Sigmund Freud say about that?"

Smiling, she said, "I will have to consult my books. I'm sure I'll find some sort of explanation. Perhaps something to do with avoiding reality and finding refuge in the mundane." Turning to the others, she said, "Now, what exactly is my role?"

"You are a relative with no income to speak of," Ernestine said.

Evie glanced at Edgar and thought he looked rather apologetic. Remembering Phillipa's remark, Evie said, "From what I understand, Lord Edgar has taken pity on me."

Ernestine nodded while Edgar looked anywhere but at Evie.

Evie considered waiting for a better time to break the news about Mrs. Sheffield. She looked around the table. Everyone looked relaxed and relatively content. So much so, she entertained the idea of postponing the task. But if she didn't tell them now, then when would she do it?

"If I may have everyone's attention, please. There is something I need to tell you." One by one, they all looked at her. Clearing her throat, Evie said, "You are bound to hear all about it sooner or later, and I would much rather it came from me.

Phillipa grabbed hold of her hand. "Are you all right?"

"I haven't said anything yet."

"Yes, but… I sense you are about to share some rather bad news."

Nodding, Evie pushed the words out, "There has been an incident in the village. Mrs. Sheffield is dead."

Phillipa brightened. "Oh, excellent ad libbing. How did you ever come up with that story?"

"I'm afraid it is all too true," Evie said.

Unfortunately, everyone's excitement drowned out Evie's clarification.

Zelma Collins declared she couldn't wait to incorporate the idea into the script. "Please tell us more."

Uncertain as to how she should proceed, Evie decided to go with the flow. Scooping in a breath, she continued, "As Caro, or rather, Lady Caroline Thwaites and I made our way to the dressmaker's store this morning, we saw…" Looking at their eager faces, she fully embraced the idea of mixing reality with fiction. "We saw the dowager coming out of the store and later we learned she had been questioned by the police."

Edgar set his glass of wine down. "Mrs. Sheffield is dead?"

Phillipa nodded. "Come now, Cousin Edgar. Do try to keep up." Leaning toward Evie, she murmured, "Lord Edgar is rather slow at times. We thought it would be a quaint character trait."

"Yes, she is dead," Evie confirmed. "I'm afraid I have no other details. Lady Carolina and I spent the rest of the morning comforting the dowager." She looked around the table and realized Caro was missing out on the ad libbing. Signaling to a footman, she asked him to find Caro. "Please ask her to join us in the dining room."

Overhearing her, Phillipa said, "My goodness. Your generosity knows no bounds."

"I'm afraid I harbor ulterior motives," Evie admitted. "If Caro learns of Edgar's inclusion, she might resent me for not inviting her to join us. And you know what happens when Caro is displeased with me."

Phillipa laughed. "Sometimes I wonder if you forget Caro is your maid."

"I prefer to live in harmony. When she arrives, please remember to address her as Carolina." Evie glanced at Tom who appeared to be minding his own business. "Have you been roped in to play a role?" she whispered.

Tom chortled. "I have no idea what is going on and I would like it to remain that way."

Edgar cleared his throat. "How did the dowager take the news of Mrs. Sheffield's death?"

"Oh, thank you for reminding me. The dowager doesn't know about Mrs. Sheffield's death and I would like to keep it that way for the time being at least."

"Yes, but... Has the dowager been implicated in the death?" Edgar asked.

Eve remembered she had related the story as a fictional account. Or, rather, everyone had assumed she had been ad libbing so she had decided to go with the flow

The scriptwriters looked from Edgar to Evie and then whispered among themselves. Heaven only knew what they planned to do with that information.

Evie lifted her chin and declared, "The dowager is in

no way involved. She merely happened to be in the wrong place, at the wrong time."

Edgar shot to his feet at the same time as the door opened. Swinging around, Evie saw the dowager entering and stopping at the door, her gaze sweeping around the room.

"My apologies, Evangeline. I have changed my mind. When I reached my room, I decided I would prefer to be among company... But now I see I might have interrupted something."

Edgar stepped back from his chair and directed the footmen to set a place for the dowager.

"Henrietta," Evie said. "We have been experimenting. Edgar has been asked to play a role in the play..." With everything that had been going on, Evie couldn't remember if she had given the dowager all the details. In case she hadn't, she decided to fill in the gaps. "He is Lord Edgar."

"Oh, my goodness." Henrietta clapped her hands. "What fun. Can I join in?"

Evie sent her gaze skating across the table. She hoped everyone remembered to avoid mentioning Mrs. Sheffield's death.

"Of course." She looked at the scriptwriters. Fearing they might turn the dowager into a servant or a mad interloper, Evie chose a role for her. "I suppose you could be the dowager."

Henrietta gave her a bright smile. "Oh, that should be easy enough. I have years of experience playing the role. How am I related to Lord Edgar?"

"You could be cousins," Evie suggested.

Taking her place next to Edgar, Henrietta looked at Tom. "And who are you playing?"

"I am merely a bystander, my lady."

"Oh, that is a marvelous idea," Zelma Collins said. "You are an unnamed character who is present in every scene, there to witness it all without commenting. A silent bystander. Modern theater at its best."

The others all nodded and Bernie piped in, "Yes. I love it. It would be like having a member of the audience up on the stage."

"So, do I have any lines?" Henrietta asked.

"We're making it all up as we go," Bernie said.

"Yes, but…" Henrietta looked slightly confused. "Surely, I should receive some sort of direction from the director of the play."

Bernie leaned forward. "Well, how do you think the dowager would react to the news of a murder taking place in the village?"

Evie stiffened. So much for warning them to avoid the subject.

"I should think she would be shocked," Henrietta said.

Zelma sat back and gazed up at the ceiling. "We need a name for the murder victim."

Henrietta glanced at Evie. "A few days ago, I would have suggested Mrs. Sheffield, but that would be in poor taste."

And too close to the truth, Evie thought.

"Mrs. Hatfield," Zelma suggested.

Evie shifted in her seat. She wanted to object to the use of the name but the others all seemed to be in agreement, including Henrietta.

"That sounds ideal. I must say, I'm ever so glad I decided to join you for lunch."

Just as they were all turning their attention to the first course, Caro made an appearance.

"I came as soon as I heard," Caro said, her tone breathless.

Evie tried to catch Henrietta's attention but the dowager sat transfixed as she watched the footmen rushing about to set a place for Caro.

"It seems I have much to catch up on," Henrietta mused. Looking at Caro, she asked, "And who are you playing?"

Caro gave her a wide grin. "I am Lady Carolina Thwaites, my lady."

"And are we related?"

Caro nodded. "Yes, I think we are all related." Looking around her, she asked, "What have I missed?"

Zelma filled her in, saying, "We have chosen a victim. She lives in the village. Her name is Mrs. Hatfield."

Caro exchanged a look with Evie that spoke of surprise.

As the others tossed around some more names for characters who might or might not be used, Evie pushed her food around the plate. Going along with the play had seemed like a good idea, now she wasn't so sure.

Out of the corner of her eye, she saw one of the footman nudge the other and signal toward the French doors leading out to the patio.

Tom, too, must have seen the gesture. They both turned discreetly and looked out onto the garden where they saw a woman approaching. Her steps faltered and she stopped on the edge of the patio. She looked around her, stumbled back and then took a decisive step forward. Bending down, she grabbed a handful of gravel and…

Evie responded with a resounding, "Oh, oh… my…"

"Stay here." Tom surged to his feet and hurried toward the French doors even as the woman's arm flung back and swiftly forward, releasing the gravel which then showered against the windows.

Everyone turned.

"Murderer!" the woman called out and then wailed her accusation again. "Murderer."

"Oh," Henrietta exclaimed. "Is this part of the entertainment too? I say, you have gone to a great deal of trouble. It is so authentic."

Tom rushed out and reached the woman in time to stop her from flinging another handful of gravel.

It took a moment for Evie to realize she had her hand pressed against her chest as if it could ease the panic surging through her. She managed to get up but she had to take a moment to make sure her legs would hold her.

Evie had never felt so cowardly as she did that moment. She didn't want to go outside but she knew she had to if she wanted to find out the reason for the woman's outburst.

Tom stood in front of the woman, his hands stretched out by his sides in an effort to stop another outburst.

"Please calm down, ma'am," he drawled out in his New England accent.

"I will do no such thing. You are harboring a murderer," the woman declared. "And I will see she is brought to justice. Mark my word, I will do it, if it's the last thing I do."

"What is the meaning of this?" Evie asked, her tone not quite as commanding as she would have liked.

The woman wore a beige dress suitable for a day walking in the spring sunshine. The rim of her straw hat cast a shadow over her eyes, but Evie could tell they were narrowed. She looked significantly older than Evie.

Looking into the distance, Evie saw some estate workers rushing toward the house. She guessed they had witnessed the commotion and wanted to help.

"Ma'am, please calm down," Tom said.

Evie groaned under her breath. She could see the woman's jaw muscles crunching and could almost feel sympathy for her. No woman liked to be told to calm down, certainly not when they were in the midst of a raging storm.

"You all think you own the place and you can do as you please. Well, I'm here to tell you things will change, starting with the police taking that woman into custody so she can answer for her crimes…"

Tom took a step forward, his arms still stretched out as if trying to herd the woman away. To her credit, the woman held her ground for as long as she could and then took a stumbling step back.

Evie rushed forward. "Clearly, you have some grievances. What is your name?"

The woman's lips parted slightly. "Anna. Anna Weston."

Evie could see the estate workers closing in. She didn't want the situation getting out of hand. At a guess, she's say Anna Weston had known the deceased. Taking a chance, she said, "You were acquainted with Mrs. Sheffield."

Anna Weston gave a stiff nod of her head. "Such a

kind-hearted soul. Everyone in the village knows what the dowager did."

"They had a disagreement. Nothing else happened," Evie reasoned.

Anna Weston's eyes narrowed. Her mouth tightened with rage. "She killed her."

Chapter Nine

The timely arrival of the police put an end to Anna Weston's public display. A constable took care of escorting her back to the village, leaving Evie and Tom to deal with the detective whose appearance on the scene had made everything all too real.

Evie dropped her gaze to the ground and studied the track marks left by Anna Weston.

She had made quite a show of protesting, digging her heels in and insisting the police take the dowager into custody.

Evie drew in a quivery breath and looked at the detective.

Mrs. Sheffield had died and the police were looking into her death.

What did that mean? Evie heard the question bouncing around her mind and refused to acknowledge it because she already knew what it meant.

The constables had come to restore the peace.

However, the detective had come on an entirely different matter.

Mrs. Sheffield had died under suspicious circumstances. Or, worse…

Evie firmed her lips. She refused to accept Henrietta could be in anyway involved or, heaven help her, responsible for the woman's death.

She studied the man who now stood in front of her, his hat in hand. A head taller than Evie, he wore a plain brown suit and black shoes polished to a high sheen. His light brown necktie sat slightly askew. Evie had to fight the urge to straighten it.

He had smiling eyes with the edges slightly crinkled as if to suggest he smiled or laughed a great deal, something that struck Evie as odd. Surely a man of the law should have hard, calculating eyes.

"I'm sorry." Evie brushed a hand across her face. "I didn't catch your name."

"Detective Inspector Jon Chambers. My apologies for the intrusion, Lady Woodridge. I believe the Dowager Countess of Woodridge is currently residing here."

And he believed that because he had already stopped by the dower house, Evie reasoned. Had the neighbors seen him? Were they now speculating and spreading the word around?

Evie drew in a calming breath. At least, the intention to calm herself had been there, but after several seconds she felt anything but calm. "Yes, that is correct."

"We should like to have a word with her, if that is convenient."

Evie suspected the detective did not wish to wait for a

convenient moment. In fact, his firm stance suggested he would not budge until he spoke with the dowager.

Evie wanted to protest, saying the police had already spoken with Henrietta, but if she looked past his smiling eyes, she could see determination written all over his face. The man would not back down.

Regardless, Evie decided to exercise her right of refusal. "I'm afraid that is not possible at the moment. The dowager is indisposed. She has strict orders from the doctor to rest."

"And I'm afraid I will have to insist," the detective said, his voice smooth and annoyingly friendly.

Evie gave him a warm smile. "In that case, we have reached an impasse. In order to enter Halton House, you will need to get past me."

He held her gaze for a moment and then dropped it. Evie imagined him trying to change his tactics. She understood he had been sent to perform his duty but she also knew he would tread with care.

Evie didn't wish to make his job difficult, but she couldn't forget she had a duty to her family. "Where is Detective Inspector O'Neill?" she asked.

"He's on another case, my lady."

Evie decided to take exception to the small smile he offered. It seemed to suggest she had no option but to deal with him and him alone.

Hearing the sound of tentative footsteps behind her, Evie closed her eyes and prayed the dowager had not taken it upon herself to see what all the fuss was about.

"Evangeline."

So much for praying, Evie thought. Turning, she gave the dowager a reassuring smile. Instead of the frailty she had seen earlier, Evie perceived something entirely different now.

Henrietta turned her attention to the detective. As she studied him, she seemed to rise in height. Her shoulders squared and her chin lifted.

"And who is this?" Henrietta asked.

He introduced himself. "Detective Inspector Jon Chambers, Lady Woodridge. My apologies for imposing on you. I hope this isn't an inconvenient time…"

"A detective?"

"Yes, my lady."

"And you wish to speak with me?"

"We are right in the middle of luncheon," Evie interjected.

Henrietta placed her hand on Evie's. "Evangeline, the detective clearly has some pressing need to speak with me. I think we should do our best to accommodate him. Would you mind terribly if we make use of one of your drawing rooms?"

"If you wish, but I would like to be present," Evie said.

The dowager patted her hand. "And I will appreciate your moral support."

Evie couldn't be entirely sure, but she suspected the dowager had just assumed an air of abject resignation.

Tom didn't bother asking for permission. He simply followed them.

They moved away from the French doors, leaving the others to speculate and, quite possibly, use what they had just witnessed to write the next scene in the play.

Instead of entering the house by the next set of doors, which would have led them directly to the morning drawing room, Evie guided the group toward the main entrance.

She needed the extra time to organize her thoughts and placate her obvious misgivings. She did not care for the intrusion, even if she understood the police had a job to do. The fact Henrietta had been singled out to answer questions annoyed Evie. She simply could not see how the dowager could assist the detective.

A footman stood at attention by the front door. Evie had no doubt Edgar had acted with swift promptness, directing someone to stand there.

"Right this way," Evie gestured and walked on ahead to the drawing room. Half way there, she changed her mind. "Perhaps we would be more comfortable in the library." Although, her intention was not to make the detective more comfortable. On the contrary. For the first time since becoming the Countess of Woodridge, Evie wanted to flaunt her good standing in society and impress the detective with the grandiosity of the house.

They crossed the entrance hall with its marble checkerboard floor, high ceiling, carved columns and grand staircase leading up to the balcony. The portraits of all the Woodridge ancestors gazed down at them from their prominent places, their expressions varying from austere to… downright humorous.

The second Earl's cheerful disposition had been remarked upon many times, with stories handed down from generation to generation about his mischievous nature.

Wishing to impress the detective with the powerful lineage, Evie guided him away from the second Earl.

She saw a footman rush to the door to take his place.

He stood with his shoulders pushed back, his spine straightened, his chin lifted and his mouth set into a grim line.

Definitely Edgar's doing, she thought. If given enough time, she had no doubt Edgar would have directed the footmen to dress in full livery. Her precious butler had read the situation and had acted with razor sharp efficiency.

At Evie's invitation, Henrietta preceded everyone into the library.

When Henrietta settled down on a high-backed chair, Evie invited the detective to sit on the sofa opposite while she stood by the fireplace next to Henrietta's chair, presenting a united front, Evie thought.

Tom bypassed the sofa and went to stand by the large stone fireplace.

Henrietta cleared her throat. "You may begin your interrogation."

The detective gave her a brisk smile. "Begging your pardon, my lady. I am not here to subject you to a hard line of questioning. I merely wish to get some facts straightened out." He drew out a notebook and flipped through the pages. "One of the constables spoke with you earlier."

"That is correct," Henrietta said.

"You claimed to have been involved in an altercation."

Henrietta nodded.

"Verbal or physical?"

Evie took a step forward. "Detective, you are addressing the Dowager Countess of Woodridge."

"With all due respect, my lady, we could be doing this down at the police station."

"What possible reason could you have to pursue such a line of questioning?" Evie demanded.

"According to an eyewitness, Lady Woodridge used her parasol to attack Mrs. Sheffield."

"Nonsense," Evie declared.

Henrietta employed her most commanding tone to say, "If I may be permitted to speak, I used my parasol to ward off an attack. In other words, I defended myself. Your so-called witness appears to be suffering from confusion. I don't particularly blame her. The entire episode transpired during a few seconds."

"I don't suppose you would care to offer a demonstration…"

Henrietta stood up. "Very well. I shall need a parasol."

Evie gave her a worried look.

"The man wants a demonstration, Evangeline, so I shall give him one," Henrietta insisted. "I see no harm in it."

None whatsoever, Evie thought, meeting with resistance as she tried to stifle her rising concerns. What if the dowager proved to be so skillful with… the parasol, the detective decided she could be responsible for whatever had happened to Mrs. Sheffield?

Evie walked over to the door and instructed the footman to find a parasol.

"Bring two," Henrietta called out. Looking at the detective, she added, "We should do this properly."

Evie returned, carrying the proposed weapons. Henrietta took one and, after a moment's hesitation, exchanged it for the other one.

"That shade doesn't quite match my gown." Taking a step back, she slashed the air with her parasol.

Evie half expected her to say *en garde*! "What would you like me to do?" she asked in a small voice.

"Swing your parasol with the intention of hitting me," Henrietta said and glanced over at the detective. "I am trying my best to re-create the scene for you."

The moment Evie swung her parasol at Henrietta, the dowager lifted her parasol and, sure enough, she managed to intercept Evie's blow.

Henrietta stepped back and explained, "Surprised by my defensive move, Mrs. Sheffield gasped and then shrieked. That's when Mrs. Green tried to intervene and she walked straight into Mrs. Sheffield's fist. As a consequence, Mrs. Sheffield then collapsed onto a chair."

"Did anyone else witness the altercation?" the detective asked.

"No, there were only the three of us present. At least, that I know of."

Evie set her parasol down and wondered why Mrs. Green had given a different account of the event. Assuming she had been the eyewitness. Had someone else been present? Perhaps one of the seamstresses or Mrs. Green's new dressmaker. They might have been hovering nearby...

"Detective," Evie said, "I believe we are entitled to know why you are investigating this matter."

He tapped his pen on his notebook. "Mrs. Sheffield's family are in a state of shock and in need of answers."

"Evie?" Henrietta shifted to the edge of her chair. "What is he talking about?"

Oh, heavens...

Evie turned and faced the dowager. "Henrietta. I don't know how to break it to you, so I am just going to come straight out and say it. Mrs. Sheffield is dead. I believe she died shortly after you left Mrs. Green's establishment."

Henrietta blinked. "Oh. Oh… I see."

"Are you all right?" Evie asked.

"Well, yes… I mean, I'm sure I had nothing to do with her death."

"Of course, you didn't. This is nothing but a misunderstanding and you… you happened to be in the wrong place, at the wrong time."

Henrietta straightened. "Well, then… Carry on. We must get to the bottom of this."

Evie turned to the detective. "Our heartfelt condolences go to the family but I fail to see what the dowager has to do with Mrs. Sheffield's death. Indeed, how did Mrs. Sheffield die?"

"We are still trying to establish that," the detective said. "Since Lady Woodridge was one of the few people to have last seen Mrs. Sheffield alive, we'd rather hoped she might be able throw some light on the matter."

"As I demonstrated, my parasol came into contact with Mrs. Sheffield's parasol," Henrietta explained, "I can't imagine how that would have brought about her demise. If she had a weak constitution, then it might have been more sensible for her to avoid any type of confrontation, but that is neither here nor there. Will you be taking me into custody?"

Instead of answering her, the detective asked, "Had there been a history of friction between you and Mrs. Sheffield?"

"Not until this morning. Although…" Henrietta glanced away.

Evie braced herself. If she spoke up, she might make

matters worse. However, if she remained silent, she could be accused of hindering the investigation. "I really don't see what this might have to do with Mrs. Sheffield's death," Evie said and then proceeded to give the detective an abbreviated version of Mrs. Sheffield's remarks during Mrs. Ellington's farewell afternoon tea. "She had made a point of questioning the way I express myself."

Henrietta stood up and stepped forward. "Lady Woodridge came under fire. While she chose to turn a blind eye to it, I decided to put a stop to it."

The detective studied the dowager for a long moment before saying, "That's when you confronted Mrs. Sheffield."

"Detective, are you trying to misinterpret my actions? I defended the honor of this family and I would do it again."

"Exactly how far would you go?" the detective asked.

"I will not dignify the question with a response."

Chapter Ten

Where were we...?

Saying he had all the information he needed, the detective thanked them for their time and left.

Henrietta turned to Evie. "Mrs. Sheffield is dead. My goodness." Her gaze dropped to her hands and then she looked up again. "How long have you known?"

"We heard the sirens just as we arrived at the dower house and then Tom and Caro confirmed it."

"And you didn't think to tell me?"

"I didn't see the point in worrying you. Would you like me to ring for some tea?"

"No, dear. It will take more than tea for me to digest this information. As for the consequences..." Henrietta found the nearest chair and sat down, her parasol still in her hand. "Time will tell."

Consequences? They had already seen Anna Weston in action. Would others follow?

"Well, despite everything, I found myself rather entertained by the process. Evangeline, what do you think the detective will do with the information we supplied him with? How can Mrs. Sheffield's family find any satisfaction in my account of the confrontation?"

"I can't even begin to imagine, Henrietta. All I can say is that they can't possibly hold you responsible for her death."

"Do you think the detective will try to trick me into doing something wrong?" Henrietta asked, her voice full of concern. "He might wish to prove I have a combative nature which needs to be brought under control."

"Henrietta..." Evie couldn't help smiling. She'd only now discovered the dowager's ability to defend herself with something other than words. Never in a million years would she have imagined the dowager acting with such swiftness. "You haven't exactly been flaunting your hidden talent. And I think you proved your point. You only acted in self-defense. If such actions were part of your nature, then we would see them displayed with greater frequency."

Henrietta didn't look convinced. "I hear say there is safety in numbers. I'm glad you invited me here to stay. I only hope it does not cast doubt on my behavior. I wouldn't wish people to think I am in hiding."

Evie sighed. "I do wish you wouldn't worry, Henrietta. I'm sure we will soon hear about Mrs. Sheffield suffering from some sort of malaise."

Henrietta studied her parasol for a moment and then set it aside.

Evie imagined she wanted to put this entire day behind her too.

"Thank you for your support, Evangeline. Now, I wish to join the others to see if they have made any progress with the play. I think it would be best if I kept myself entertained with other thoughts."

When the dowager left, Evie collapsed into the nearest chair. "What did you make of all that?" she asked Tom.

"I'm more interested to know what you're thinking," he said.

"Well, on the one hand, the detective might have been seeking clarification. And, on the other hand, he could have been trying to pin Mrs. Sheffield's death on someone." Evie brushed her hand across her brow. Lowering her voice, she said, "I hope that's the end of it."

"You seem to have forgotten about Anna Weston."

Evie sat up. "While I don't wish to make excuses for her behavior, I assume she'd been overcome with grief. Surely, her accusations cannot be substantiated. What am I saying? Of course they can't be proven because Henrietta did not kill Mrs. Sheffield."

"I take it you've never seen her before."

Evie gave a small shrug. "I might have seen her at Sunday service or around the village. I can't say that I have ever had a conversation with Anna Weston. I'm more likely to remember a person if I engage them in even the briefest chat. I'll ask Caro. She might know something about her, and if she doesn't, I'm sure she could find something out." Unable to stop fidgeting, Evie brushed her fingers across her eyes. "Actually, forget I said that. I'd prefer to put this unpleasant business behind us. Let's hope that's the last we see of the detective and Anna Weston. I have enough to keep me occupied, or should that be preoccupied?" Getting up, she added, "Henrietta had the right idea. Perhaps I should go see what the playwrights are up to. We might be in time for some coffee."

"Then again," Tom said, "this is your home and you can ask for coffee whenever you want some."

"True. However, the household staff have their lunch after us. I don't like to bother them. We might have to wait a while."

They found everyone had already settled down in the drawing room. When Evie saw Henrietta, she came to a swift halt.

Henrietta stood in the middle of the room where she had commandeered everyone's attention. "I have an announcement to make. Ah, Evangeline. I'm glad you are here. You can help me answer some questions as I'm sure everyone is bound to be curious about the current state of affairs."

Evie tried to speak but the words simply wouldn't take shape so she offered a smile.

"As I was saying," the dowager continued, "I have been interrogated by the police in relation to Mrs. Sheffield's death. Despite the detective being satisfied with my responses, I believe I am now the number one suspect."

Exclamations of surprise swept around the room.

"I should like to make a suggestion some of you might find outrageous."

Oh, dear. Evie wondered if she should draw the dowager aside before she did or said something that couldn't be... unsaid or undone.

Henrietta struck up an imperious pose. She could not

have commanded more attention if she had stood on a dais, holding a golden scepter and wearing a crown.

"I think we might now take the liberty of changing our fictional victim's name to Mrs. Sheffield." Looking at Evie, the dowager added, "I also think the scriptwriters might assist us in solving this mystery."

Evie took a tentative step forward, her tone beseeching as she said, "There is no mystery, Henrietta."

"Isn't there? I beg to differ. Perhaps you failed to notice the detective did not mention a cause of death." The dowager shuddered. "To think I am probably the last person to have seen Mrs. Sheffield alive."

"The dowager makes a valid point," Tom said under his breath.

"Yes," Evie agreed. So much for putting everything behind them. Evie considered changing the subject. However, she didn't wish to diminish the dowager's obvious concerns. Before she could stop herself, she asked, "Can you remember what happened when you left Mrs. Green's establishment?"

Henrietta pressed her hand against her collar. "How could I forget? All those people just standing there like vultures waiting to peck at the remains of my shattered reputation."

"My apologies, Henrietta. I should have been more specific. I am referring to the moment before you actually exited the store. You said Mrs. Sheffield had collapsed."

"Oh, yes. Despite the blow she received to her face, Mrs. Green stood by, fanning Mrs. Sheffield. I believe she also called out to someone. Let me think… Abigail."

Mrs. Green's new employee.

"When Abigail appeared, Mrs. Green withdrew into

the back room. Perhaps that is when she telephoned the police. They arrived soon after and questioned me. Mrs. Sheffield groaned and moaned throughout it all. I believe she might have been trying to overstate her condition. Then, I made my exit. As I did, I restrained myself. In my opinion, I would have been well within my rights to deliver a parting shot, but I felt it would have been in poor taste. Instead, I chose the high ground. In any case, Mrs. Sheffield had still been alive. I know that because I distinctly heard her continuing to moan and groan."

Evie realized she was still standing by the door. That made her wonder about Abigail. Had the dressmaker's assistant been standing nearby? Perhaps close enough to have seen everything or at least something of significance? Was she the witness the detective had mentioned?

The fact no one had asked any questions suggested they were all in a state of stunned disbelief. They remained attentive; captivated by Henrietta as if they were seeing her for the first time or, at least, in a different light. Reading their expressions, Evie could see varying states of surprise and perhaps intrigue.

As the hostess, she felt inclined to lighten the mood.

Making a beeline for a chair, Evie tried to change the subject. "I hope you were all able to resume your meal."

"Hardly," Phillipa said. She looked around at the others as if seeking consent. The scriptwriters all nodded. "Who was that woman and why did she accuse the dowager of being a murderer?"

"It was nothing but a misunderstanding," Evie assured her. "Her name is Anna Weston. I'm afraid that is all we know about her."

Edgar cleared his throat.

"Edgar, is there something you wish to say?" Henrietta asked.

"Well, my lady… It is not really my place…"

"Perhaps we should speak with Lord Edgar," Henrietta suggested. "Would that make you more inclined to share what you know?"

Giving the dowager a whimsical smile, Edgar lifted his chin and said, "I do believe I have some knowledge which might throw some light on Miss Weston's behavior."

Everyone shifted slightly, their attention moving from the dowager to Edgar.

When he didn't speak, Henrietta said, "Would you prefer to take center stage?"

Without further encouragement, Edgar took a couple of steps and went to stand in front of the fireplace. Lifting his chin, he declared, "Miss Anna Weston has lived in the village of Halton all her life."

"That's it?" Evie whispered.

"Weston Cottage, near the vicarage?" Henrietta asked.

"I believe so, yes."

"I thought the family had moved away," Henrietta mused.

"The head of the family passed away several years ago. I believe his widow remarried and left her daughter, Anna Weston, the cottage."

Henrietta asked, "Are you saying she is a spinster?"

Edgar's cheeks colored slightly. "Well, yes. She has never married so I suppose that makes her a spinster."

Evie tilted her head in thought. How had Edgar come by all that information? He'd only been at Halton House for a short while…

Not bothering to hide her impatience, Henrietta pressed

him for more details. "Does she live alone? Is she involved in the community? I can't say that I have come across her."

"I believe she tends to keep to herself." Edgar clasped his hands and then wrung them together. "If memory serves, she entered the annual flower show once but did not take a ribbon."

"Would you say the experience left her embittered?" the dowager asked.

Evie looked at Tom in time to catch his surprised expression.

He edged toward her and murmured, "The dowager is putting the detective to shame."

They both tuned in to hear Edgar's reply.

"Embittered? I don't know her well enough to make such a claim. In fact, I don't know her at all, my lady."

"Cousin Henrietta to you, sir. Remember, you are Lord Edgar."

Tom's chest shook with suppressed laughter.

Evie glanced around the room and saw everyone else barely containing their amusement.

"Of course, Cousin Henrietta. Perhaps I could employ the assistance of some of the downstairs staff. They might be able to gain further information which might prove to be useful. After all, we cannot have your name tarnished for no good reason." His eyebrows hitched up slightly. "That is to say... Assuming we have no reason to be concerned..."

It took a moment for the dowager to grasp the full meaning of his remark. When she did, Henrietta huffed and could not have sounded more offended as she spoke, "I have no idea what you are implying, Cousin Edgar."

Tom backed away from the room. Glancing over her shoulder, Evie saw him bending over with laughter.

When he returned to the drawing room, his eyes glittered and he could barely suppress his smile.

"Regarding my earlier announcement," the dowager said, "I should like to make it plainly clear." She glanced around the drawing room until she was sure she had everyone's full attention. "I am innocent of any and all wrongdoing. My actions were motivated by the need to preserve this family's good name and good standing in our community. That does not mean I would resort to committing a grievous act of violence."

Silence followed her declaration.

Evie could have sworn she heard her heart beating.

Suddenly, Zelma Collins surged to her feet and clapped as she exclaimed, "*Brava. Bravissima.*"

"Oh." Henrietta's cheeks colored. She pressed her hand to her throat. "I always thought that exclamation was reserved for exceptionally good operatic performances, but I'll take what I can." She made a deep bow.

"May we have leave to use your lines in our play, my lady?" Zelma Collins asked.

"Certainly, but I would like to have the opportunity to peruse the final work."

"As you wish." Zelma resumed her place and wasted no time noting down her ideas.

"If you like, I could also give you a demonstration of the steps I took to defend the family honor." The dowager glanced at Evie. "We shall need those parasols again, Evangeline…"

"Oh… Could we perhaps postpone that until this evening?" Evie asked.

"Yes, that might be wise. Performing is thirsty work." The dowager glanced around and caught the attention of a footman. "Could we possibly have some tea, please? Oh, and could I also trouble you for something to nibble on. Some sandwiches, perhaps. Nothing too elaborate."

Evie tried to remember the footman's name… "Benjamin, could you ask cook to prepare a small platter, please. At her convenience, of course. I think we could all do with some sustenance."

Waving a piece of paper in the air, Zelma Collins rushed up to Edgar and appeared to confer with him. While she spoke, he nodded and when he spoke, she nodded. Then, Edgar brushed his finger across his chin as if in thought and, pointing to the page Zelma held, said something that made Zelma jump with excitement.

"If you want my opinion," Tom murmured, "I think you have just been made the scapegoat."

Evie gasped. Her eyes widened with surprise. "Why would you say that?"

Tom's shoulder lifted into a casual shrug. "You're the poor relation. That makes you superfluous."

"But that is horrible."

"It's a harsh reality. Women of little substance tend to be overlooked by society. At least, that's the impression I got when I read Jane Austen."

"You've read Jane Austen?"

Tom folded his arms. "Why are you so surprised?"

"It simply doesn't strike me as the type of book a man would be interested in reading."

"And yet, every drawing room I walk into appears to have a book by Jane Austen lying about." Tom hitched his head toward a side table.

"Oh, yes. I see your point." If memory served, Henrietta had a copy of *Pride and Prejudice* on her desk. "Anyhow, I take offense."

Tom smiled. "And so, you should."

"Money is not everything," Evie said.

"It is if you have to feed and clothe yourself." He looked around. "And keep the roof from falling on you. Houses such as this one require a great deal to maintain it."

True. She knew many people who had married for the singular purpose of acquiring a fortune. "If I am ejected from this house, I shall... I shall look for a position. I could become a lady's companion or perhaps a tutor..."

Tom glanced at her and gave her a worried look. "I hope you realize I am referring to your character in the play."

"Of course, and I am doing my best to step into character. After all, I wouldn't want to disappoint my guests."

"I see. And what does the fictional Evie Parker excel at doing?"

"Well..." Nothing came to mind. Evie cringed. What did that mean? If she were to be stripped of her wealth and title, would she land on her feet? "I'm sure I could be a lady's companion."

"Are you sure?" Tom asked.

"I believe you are teasing me."

His eyes crinkled at the edges.

The footman's arrival served as a timely distraction. When he set a tray with a pot of tea and sandwiches down on a table, Evie acted with uncharacteristic promptness.

"As the poor relation, I am going to be uncouth and serve myself first. Who knows? This might be my last meal before I am hauled away to prison because my fictional hoity-toity relatives have chosen to throw me to the wolves."

Settling down with a cup of tea and a sandwich to make up for the meal she'd had to abandon, she glanced around the drawing room, only then noticing Caro's absence. "Where is Caro?"

Phillipa came to sit beside her and said, "Oh, a footman came in a while ago and told her Millicent had arrived and needed to be collected from the train station. Caro wanted to go along and make sure she would settle in properly."

Heavens, she'd forgotten about Millicent. "Will you all excuse me, please, I have another matter to attend to." Ignoring Tom's raised eyebrow, she exited the drawing room and made her way up the main stairs, along the way smiling up at the 2nd Earl of Woodridge.

Since Caro had missed out on getting a new dress, Evie wanted to go through her wardrobe and select something for her to wear during rehearsals.

Her plans, however, were derailed when she encountered Caro and Millicent in the hallway.

"We were just coming down, milady," Caro said.

Millicent grinned. "I wanted to eavesdrop on the play. It sounds ever so exciting."

"How was your train journey, Millicent?" Evie asked.

"Oh, I enjoyed it tremendously, milady."

"Thank you for coming at such short notice," Evie said as they made their way to her boudoir.

When Caro asked her for news about the woman who had disrupted their lunch, Evie filled her in and included details about the interview with the detective.

"This odd business with Miss Anna Weston and the

detective has left me wondering what the villagers are talking about," Evie remarked.

Millicent and Caro exchanged a look that spoke of conspiracy.

Finally, Caro said, "I told Millicent about me going to the village while you kept the dowager company."

Millicent's pale blue eyes brightened with a hint of excitement. "I must admit, I feel jealous. I wish I could do something as daring as that."

As Evie pushed the door to her chamber open, a footman walked by and Evie thought she heard Millicent giggling.

Evie turned in time to see Caro elbowing Millicent and shooting her a warning look to behave.

Evie refrained from commenting. Her town maid had a reputation for admiring good looking young men from a distance and Evie didn't see any harm in that. Although, she did tend to prattle on about them, which could become tedious.

"Milady, I hope I'm not being presumptuous," Millicent said.

Evie encouraged her with a smile.

"Would you like me to go to the village? I could eavesdrop on people's conversations."

"You want to spy for me?" Evie gave a slow shake of her head. "That sounds rather underhanded."

"Wouldn't you like to know what people are saying? From what Caro told me, one person has already made an attempt to cast aspersions on her ladyship. In your place, I wouldn't be able to sleep. What if the villagers decide to organize themselves and storm Halton House?"

"She does have a point, milady," Caro said. "It might

all sound far-fetched but one never knows. I doubt any of us expected that woman to stand on your lawn making false accusations."

"True," Evie mused. "But I'm sure Anna Weston acted impulsively."

"She didn't look at all pleased when the police escorted her away," Caro offered. "What if she decides to take matters further? She might try to incite the villagers into taking action." Caro lowered her voice to a hushed whisper. "There is power in numbers."

Millicent nodded. "In your place, I would want to be sure."

Evie couldn't see any reason why she couldn't go along with the idea. Millicent worked at the London house and had only been to Halton House a couple of times. "Did you ever go to the village during your visits here?" Evie asked.

"No, milady. I've thought it through. No one will recognize me. If I happen to wander around and… perhaps drop in on the various stores, I could maybe find out what people are talking about without anyone linking me to Halton House."

"What if someone asks where you're from?" Evie knew the local villagers liked nothing better than to keep their village safe. If anyone new showed up, someone was bound to notice and make sure they meant no harm.

"Oh, that hadn't occurred to me." Millicent's lips turned downward. She could not have looked more disappointed.

Evie gave her a bright smile. "You could tell them you are visiting someone in the area…" It couldn't be anyone from Halton House because then her loyalty would be called into question.

"Mrs. Esther Higgins is away," Caro said. "She's quite elderly and is hard of hearing so she rarely talks with anyone. She's visiting her granddaughter who lives in Bath. Millicent could say she is a distant relative and here to look after her house and her cat."

"Does Mrs. Higgins have a cat?" Evie asked.

Caro nodded. "She does, indeed, and Edmonds, the chauffeur, has been dropping in every day to feed it."

Evie hoped she didn't live to regret her decision. "That sounds like a solid plan. There, you have your cover and my approval, Millicent. Do you think you are up to it?"

Millicent gave a vigorous nod. "Oh, yes, milady. I had no idea being in the country could be so exciting…"

Chapter Eleven
―――――――――――――

When the world wearies and society fails to satisfy, there is always the garden.

The next morning, Evie woke up feeling refreshed and untethered by all the concerns which had plagued her the previous day.

Wishing for the rest of the day to continue on a smooth and steady course, she decided to leave everyone to their own devices and immediately after enjoying her breakfast in bed and dressing in a pretty floral print dress, she carried her little woven basket to the gardener's shed and equipped herself with a small garden trowel.

Settling down at her own personal garden plot near one of the drawing rooms, Evie lost herself in the simple task of turning the soil. Since she had begun working on her venture too late in the season, she only had weeds to contain, but she would eventually plant... Well, she would find something to plant.

George Mills had suggested drawing a small map of her garden plot and writing down the flowers she wished to grow. It sounded easy enough.

Glancing up, Evie brushed back a stray lock of hair. She looked across the lawn and studied the garden near one of the drawing rooms. George had explained he had planted early bloomers there to ensure there would be something to look at as early as April.

He had spoken at length about which flowers performed the best in the early spring. While Evie had tried to pay attention, she had been too eager to get started, her fingers itching to sink into the soil.

"Bluebells and daffodils," Evie murmured. Tapping her chin, she realized she would need something else growing so that when the first blooms ran through their cycle, the next ones would be ready to take over. But those flowers wouldn't come up until next spring. She needed to find something she could plant now and enjoy in summer.

Plucking out a weed, she turned her thoughts to the night before. She had no idea how she had survived an entire evening of ad-libbing. The scriptwriters had talked at great length about murder scenes in plays inspiring the others to attempt several different versions; the most enthusiastic displays focusing on Lady Macbeth's sleep-walking scene.

There had been several attempts to draw her into some of the scenes, but she had found it all too morbid. Especially so soon after Mrs. Sheffield's demise.

Henrietta had insisted Edgar needed to join them for dinner because otherwise, she risked forgetting her lines.

And, in her opinion, the more they practiced, the sooner they would solve the mystery of Mrs. Sheffield's death.

For some reason, the dowager had remained intent on believing there had to be a mystery. In her opinion, the police had singled her out because they held some sort of vital piece of information. Something far more significant than an eyewitness' account.

Evie had wanted to correct Henrietta and explain the police had only been confirming facts but the dowager had become convinced there had to be a mystery. However, her focus had turned to perfecting her lines and so the mystery had been temporarily forgotten. At least, until later in the evening…

Henrietta and Edgar had been delightful to watch. The dowager had simply played herself while Edgar had portrayed a perfect titled gentleman used to spending his time enjoying country pursuits.

As the poor relation, Evie had mostly remained in the shadows because, as Tom had pointed out, lesser members of the family were not entitled to shine.

It had suited Evie only too well. She had sat in a corner playing a game of Solitaire while enjoying the show. Evie had been particularly amused by the splendid performance put on by Caro. Or, rather, *Lady Carolina Thwaites*.

Evie had never thought she would live to see the day when someone matched Henrietta word for word. And Caro had done a fine job of it, almost outwitting the dowager. At one point, they had even sparred. Smiling, Evie remembered the parasols making another appearance.

Evie stopped her digging and looked up in time to see a flock of swallows sweeping across the park.

"There you are."

Turning, she saw Tom approaching. He had once again favored a Savile Row suit in a light shade of gray. "You've missed breakfast."

"Yes, but I just caught up with the scriptwriters. They have made progress and have decided the murder must take place in the third act. Also, as discussed last night, the victim is to die of poison."

Poison?

During the main course the previous night, they had discussed the possibility of the fictional Mrs. Sheffield being poisoned. One of the scriptwriters had come up with that suggestion. Evie couldn't remember if it had been Zelma or Bernie.

Then, Phillipa had said they had already carried out extensive research on the subject so they should be able to find an interesting poison.

By the time they had retired to the drawing room for their coffee, the conversation had shifted to motives.

The scriptwriters had been fixated on money. Henrietta had said Mrs. Sheffield had inherited a house and the surrounding land, but that hadn't yielded any real understanding of Mrs. Sheffield's circumstances.

"I do wish they'd write about something else." Evie sunk her trowel into the soil and turned it with vigor.

"Are you, by any chance, trying to avoid your guests?" Tom asked, his tone teasing.

"I'm sure they get on well enough without my assistance."

"Oh, but you have so much experience and valuable knowledge to share." Tom brushed his hand across his chin. "And others feel the same way too. Now that I think about it, Evie Parker would be the perfect poisoner. No one would suspect her because no one notices her. Wouldn't you agree?"

Evie refused to answer.

"She's as quiet as a mouse... Yes, the more I think about it, the more I'm inclined to see her as a poisoner. And, since the scriptwriters have taken direction from Henrietta, the fictional Mrs. Sheffield has been modeled on the recently deceased Mrs. Sheffield. That gives you some personal experience to tap into."

Evie's fingers tightened around the handle until her knuckles showed white. She stabbed the ground with her trowel and muttered, "Are you trying to taunt me into acting out my role?"

"Admit it. You secretly wish you'd poisoned Mrs. Sheffield."

Evie surged to her feet and waved her garden trowel. "So, I'm supposed to play the role of the family's charity case and be responsible for murdering someone. I'm not sure my character has it in her to do it."

"Doesn't she? She's been looked down on by her family and everyone she encounters. Needless to say, the fictional Mrs. Sheffield made Evie Parker's life miserable by always being condescending and belittling her in front of her family."

Evie gritted her teeth. "She asked for it."

"There, you see." Tom gave her a bright smile. "I knew you had it in you. You know what they say about confession being good for the soul."

Heavens. If she didn't go along, she'd never get any peace.

Evie spread her arms out and exclaimed, "You're right. I did poison Mrs. Sheffield. She had it coming."

A gasp had Evie stilling and Tom swinging around.

"Did you hear that?" Evie asked in a hushed tone.

"Yes." Tom's demeanor changed from fun and games to the serious business of looking after Evie. "Stay here and hold on tight to that trowel. Better still, go back inside the house."

He rounded the corner and strode off in the direction of the main entrance. Counting to five, Evie then followed him. As she rounded the corner, she saw Tom picking up his step and another man hurrying away.

Tom called out to him but the man did not stop.

Evie lifted her hand to shield her eyes from the sun. Squinting, she tried to think if she recognized the man trying to beat a hasty retreat.

He had straight sandy hair, cropped short at the back and he wore a black suit.

Even from the back, Evie could see his head appeared to be slightly thrown back. He had his back ramrod straight and his arms slightly raised as if to assist him in pushing himself to walk faster. When he broke his stride, Evie thought he looked about ready to break into a run.

Tom called out to him again, "Wait up."

Instead of trying to catch up to Tom, Evie slowed down. She tried to think who might dress in black…

Someone in mourning?

Could it be a servant, perhaps dropping off a message?

Or had one of Mrs. Sheffield's relatives come to express their grievances? Or worse, had they come to make further accusations and seek justice? What if Millicent had been right and Halton House was about to come under siege from aggrieved relatives and villagers?

She looked at him long and hard as another alternative flooded her mind.

No… He wasn't a mourner.

Evie tried to speak but only managed to produce a wheezing sound, the result of the shocking realization they were chasing after an innocent man.

Pressing her hand to her throat, she finally managed to speak, "Tom. Wait… Stop…" Then, she realized she couldn't actually call out a warning because it would sound… uncouth. Regardless, they were chasing the vicar away…

Chapter Twelve

"Where there's tea there's hope."
– Arthur Wing Pinero

*E*vie called out again, "Tom. Stop."
But Tom didn't hear her. Or worse, he had heard her but he had chosen to ignore her...

Tom must have used up all his patience. When the vicar showed no sign of stopping or even slowing down, Tom broke into a run, but at the sound of his pounding footsteps, the vicar stumbled and then broke into a run too.

That made Tom more determined. Not that he had to try very hard. Whether or not he put any effort into it, Tom had a terrific physique. Evie had no doubt he could run to the village and back without breaking into a sweat.

When he caught up to the man, he grabbed hold of his arm and pulled him back.

Evie pressed her hands against her cheeks. Heavens, she would have to apologize to the vicar even before they had been properly introduced.

Oh, how she wished she was wrong, but reason told her it had to be the vicar.

Scrambling for an acceptable explanation, one she could live with, Evie decided they'd been well within their rights in wanting to speak to the man since he had, strictly speaking, waltzed into private property without an invitation.

The entrance to the estate was nearly half a mile away. So, there must have been some sort of intention on his part and that intention could have been misconstrued by someone who hadn't known he was a vicar.

Evie tossed the idea around and then she argued that no one in their right mind would try to break into a large, fully staffed house in the middle of the day…

As much as she wanted to believe she could be wrong about the man's identity, it failed to signify.

At the end of the day, she knew he had overheard her conversation with Tom. The man had most likely come from the village so he had to know about Mrs. Sheffield's death.

This didn't look good…

Evie tried to recall her exact words. There had been something about poisoning and maybe killing…

Tom now appeared to be having a heated exchange with the man.

Evie snapped out of her stupor and rushed toward them, all the while chastising herself.

A vicar.

And not just any vicar. *The Village of Halton's new vicar.*

The one whose name she couldn't remember.

"Good morning." Evie couldn't think of anything else to say. It took all her willpower just to tear her eyes away from his white collar.

How would she survive this unforgivable *faux pas*?

The vicar's face flushed a deep shade of crimson. His light brown eyes jumped from Tom to Evie. He looked about ready to say something but then he firmed his lips and took a deep swallow.

"You're the new vicar." Evie injected as much friendliness into her voice as she could manage. The fact she couldn't remember his name put her in an awkward position. "We've been expecting you."

Instead of quelling his obvious indignation, Evie thought she had made the situation worse. Belatedly, she admitted her mistake and realized she should have started with an apology…

As the vicar straightened his jacket, he huffed out a breath and came close to glowering at Tom. He had clearly taken offense at being manhandled and appeared to be on the verge of protesting the indignity he had suffered.

If she didn't do something or say something quickly to salvage the situation and make amends, she would probably end up doing penance for the rest of her natural life.

Fortunately, the vicar appeared to change his mind. Straightening his shoulders and lifting his chin, he gave Evie an abrupt nod.

"My name is James Chatterlain. I'm the new vicar."

"My apologies," Tom said, his tone slightly on the tight side. "You appeared to be trying to run away."

"Indeed. I... I..."

Evie finally remembered her manners and extended her hand. "Reverend Chatterlain. Welcome to Halton House. I am Lady Woodridge."

His lips pursed and he hesitated for a fraction of a second before giving another stiff nod. Stretching his hand out, he shook Evie's hand. "Pleased to meet you, Lady Woodridge." He released her hand and took a deep swallow. After a few seconds, he looked down at his hand. Employing the utmost discretion, something Evie didn't fail to notice, he wiped his hand against his coat.

That's when Evie realized she had a light dusting of soil covering her fingers...

Succumbing to a feeling of awkwardness, Evie's mind went completely blank.

There were rules of behavior. Protocols to follow. Heavens, she had been brought up to deal with difficult situations. Yet, she could only fixate on the last few minutes.

Why had he tried to run away? Had he really overheard her?

"I had no idea you would be arriving so soon." Evie tucked back a stray lock of hair. "I'm sorry you didn't receive a proper welcome..." She gave him an encouraging nod, but the vicar didn't help her out with small talk. "Would you care to join us for some tea?" Evie gasped. "Heavens, I must have been in the sun too long. I've forgotten my manners. This is Mr. Tom Winchester."

The vicar gave Tom a cautious smile.

"You must come in for some tea," she urged.

"I... I didn't mean to impose on you, my lady. I had merely wished to introduce myself and... also, I wanted to thank you for your generous gift basket. A veritable cornucopia. In fact, it was quite a lavish bounty. I daresay, I will not have to worry about meals for many days to come."

"Oh, I hope you enjoy jam and marmalade." And whatever else Mrs. Horace had thought to add to the basket.

His cheeks colored a deep crimson. "As a matter of fact, I do. It was very thoughtful of you, my lady. I will not need to worry about meals for…" He broke off and wrung his hands together as he probably realized he was repeating himself.

In an effort to lighten the mood, Evie laughed. "I think I might have been somewhat presumptuous. I didn't know if there would be a Mrs. Chatterlain or not." She gestured toward the front door. "Shall we go in?"

The vicar hesitated.

Thinking he might be about to bolt, Evie glanced at Tom. Somehow, they engaged in a wordless conversation and reached a silent agreement, which required them to work in tandem.

While Evie moved toward the door, Tom herded the vicar along. Not that he had any choice, since they had sandwiched the poor man!

Evie wasted no time calling for refreshments to be brought to the morning drawing room. First impressions were vital and she had failed dismally, so it would now be up to her to reverse the damage.

Glancing at Tom, she saw him tap his nose.

Evie frowned. Was Tom trying to convey a secret message?

She handed the vicar a cup of tea and settled down opposite him. When Tom chose to stand by the window, Evie imagined he would later declare he had merely wanted to avoid causing the man further distress.

The vicar sat on the edge of his seat and glanced around. "This is a lovely room, my lady."

From the moment he'd set foot inside Halton House, the vicar had shown both interest and appreciation, expressing his delight at just about everything he saw.

"Thank you. I've always thought so too. As much as I would like to take credit, it must all go to the Dowager Countess of Woodridge. She's actually staying with us."

The vicar's cup rattled on its saucer.

"Oh, I'm sorry. Is the cup too hot to handle?" she asked, her tone full of innocent intent.

"I must say, time certainly does fly." He looked about him as if searching for a suitable place on which to deposit his teacup.

"Surely, you're not leaving so soon." He hadn't even taken a sip of his tea.

"I'm afraid I have only now remembered I am supposed to meet my new housekeeper," he said.

The door to the drawing room opened and Henrietta swept in saying, "My goodness, I can't remember the last time I had so much fun. It almost feels naughty. Evangeline, I believe the poison will work a treat." Noticing the vicar, she stopped. "Oh... I didn't realize you had company."

"Henrietta, this is our new vicar, the Reverend James Chatterlain." Recalling the conversation they'd had a couple of days before, Evie wondered if Henrietta would have preferred to seek her own introduction after she'd had the opportunity to determine if it would be a safe acquaintance or not. Although, that would have struck Evie as odd since Henrietta would be seeing the vicar every Sunday.

The dowager gave a noncommittal nod. As she settled down on the sofa, she cleared her throat, but before she could speak, the vicar surged to his feet.

"I really should be getting back." The vicar made such a hasty exodus out of the drawing room, he almost tripped over his feet as well as his words of gratitude for a wonderful welcome.

When the door closed, Evie and Tom stared at each other, their expressions confused.

Henrietta shifted from side to side, looking first at Tom and then at Evie. "What just happened?"

Evie pressed her hands to her cheeks. "I'm not sure, but I believe I now have my work cut out for me."

Henrietta leaned forward. "You have something on your nose, Evangeline, and on your cheeks."

"My... nose? My cheeks?" Evie dug inside her pocket and produced a handkerchief.

"I tried to tell you," Tom said. "It's a smudge of dirt."

"You let me sit here all that time... You should have been clearer."

"My apologies," Tom offered. "There's really no excuse... except for the fact that I became captivated by the fellow. He's an odd creature."

"Tom, would you care to explain what went on here?" Henrietta asked. "I feel I have somehow missed the joke."

Tom glanced at Evie and raised his eyebrows slightly.

"It's all right, Tom. You can tell Henrietta."

Tom grinned. "With great pleasure."

As Tom recounted the tale of how the vicar overheard their conversation and then proceeded to make a swift getaway, Evie sat back and thought about the vicar's reaction when she had mentioned the dowager's name.

What had that been about?

Chapter Thirteen

News from the village…

Needing to freshen up before lunch, Evie retired to her room. At least, she used that as an excuse. In reality, she had wanted to get away from Henrietta who had insisted she play out her admission of guilt scene.

Not once, but twice.

Henrietta's eyes had shimmered with laughter. When she had begged for another encore, Evie had feigned tiredness and had excused herself.

She hoped Henrietta wouldn't bring up the episode during luncheon.

As she entered her room, her eyes went straight to the clock on the mantle above the fireplace. Caro usually met her here without Evie having to ring for her, but Evie had broken with her routine by coming upstairs earlier than usual.

Instead of ringing for Caro, she decided to spend the time in quiet introspection. If she happened to fall asleep and missed lunch, so much the better.

Evie walked on through to her private boudoir. As she reclined on the chaise lounge, she wondered if she might be trying to hide from the world in general and, specifically, from her responsibilities. Not to mention... "Chaos."

How on earth had it found her? She had been doing so well, following a gentle routine, appreciating the small pleasures in life and never once complaining of a dull moment.

Taking a deep breath, she encouraged her mind to empty, but it simply refused to co-operate.

"Milady?"

"Oh, Caro." Evie sat up.

"My apologies if I interrupted your slumber. Would you like me to come back later?"

"No. No, please stay." Evie shifted and signaled to a chair. "You'll never believe the morning I've had. It's as if the Fates have decided to conspire against me," Evie said and gave Caro an abbreviated version of that morning's events.

"Oh, dear." Caro looked over her shoulder. "Perhaps this isn't a good time..."

"What is it, Caro?"

"Well, Millicent has just returned from the village but you seem to be under a dark cloud..."

Evie actually brightened. "But that is good news. Where is she?"

"Not far." Caro looked over her shoulder and called out, "It's safe to come in."

When Millicent entered the boudoir, Evie deepened her voice to sound like Edgar and asked, "What news do you bring from the village?"

Millicent grinned. "The new vicar has arrived, milady. Then again, you already know that. My apologies, I couldn't help overhearing your tale."

"Don't say anything until I come back." Caro stepped out of the boudoir. Moments later, she rushed back in carrying a dress for Evie to change into.

"The entire village is talking about the new vicar," Millicent continued.

Evie plumped up her cushions and sat up properly. "That's good. It means the focus has been taken off the dowager."

Millicent grimaced and glanced at Caro who gave her a nod of encouragement. "Not exactly, milady. Everyone is hoping the vicar will be able to exorcise the devil from her ladyship since she must surely be possessed. Otherwise, why would she have killed a perfectly nice lady such as Mrs. Sheffield."

"Millicent! How could you say that?" Evie exclaimed.

"Oh, but I didn't. I mean, I did just now... I supposed I should have explained. The baker's wife is the one who believes the dowager is possessed."

Evie tried to think if she had ever met the baker's wife. "Remind me what she looks like."

"Let me think." Millicent closed her eyes as if bringing the image of the baker's wife to mind. "She has ginger hair and pale blue eyes and is quite robust."

Evie didn't recall ever meeting her or even seeing her

at Sunday service. But she knew of her. At least, from a distance. Yes, she would be able to recognize her by her hair. It made no sense. Why would she say such a horrible thing? Did she have something against the dowager?

"I saw a group of people gathered outside the dressmaker's shop," Millicent continued. "They appeared to be holding some sort of vigil there. One woman held a candle and a prayer book, which I found strange because it was morning. They were talking about the new vicar and saying he would get to the bottom of it all."

Evie pressed her hands together. "Did you hear anyone talking about motive?"

"I heard one woman say her ladyship wanted to silence poor Mrs. Sheffield because she knew something about you."

Evie swung her legs off the chaise lounge. "What?"

"I shouldn't worry too much about that, milady. Someone actually jumped to your defense saying she refused to hear a bad word said about you because, since your return to the village, life has become infinitely more interesting."

"Did anyone mention pitchforks?" Caro asked.

"No." Millicent shook her head. "I'm happy to report the general feeling is that of curiosity."

Evie took a deep swallow. "About what?"

"I kept the best part until last. Mr. Sheffield is receiving visitors. It seems everyone wishes to express their condolences in person. His sister and sister in law are keeping him company. In fact, they have been staying with him for the past few weeks, which is a blessing in disguise because, otherwise, he would not know how to proceed. Anyhow, the villagers are curious to know when and if you will visit him to pay your respects. Someone mentioned a lookout but I didn't get any details because the dressmaker's maid came out and began sweeping the storefront sidewalk. I believe she wanted to encourage us to move on."

"And, did you?" Evie asked.

"Well, yes. Everyone else moved on so I had no reason to remain."

Heavens. She hadn't given any thought to paying Mr. Sheffield a visit. Since they were not acquainted, it would be perfectly acceptable to wait until the funeral service to pay her respects.

As for the lookout…

She would have to alert Tom. He could organize the estate workers to keep an eye out on anyone… keeping a lookout on the estate.

Evie put her hand on her forehead and swooned.

"Milady." Caro rushed to her side.

"Oh, I'm fine, Caro. It seems only yesterday… or the day before, I had been sitting down to tea without a care in the world. And now, everything is in disarray. Please tell me I am overreacting."

"You are overreacting, milady," Caro assured her. "Although, in my humble opinion, you do have a right to be concerned. Your arch nemesis has died at the worst possible time, under curious circumstances…"

"Caro!"

"I'm so sorry, milady. I seem to be a bit befuddled. It most likely has to do with playing the role of Lady Carolina Thwaites. I don't even have to exert myself as it seems to come quite naturally to me, however, now I'm plain Caro…"

"Oh, you're never plain, Caro."

"Thank you for saying so, milady. Anyhow, Lady Carolina, as you know, rather enjoys expressing her opinions and I feel it is not my place, as Caro, to impede her freedom of expression."

"Do you really think of Mrs. Sheffield as my foe?"

Caro gave a small nod. "I'm sure if she had lived long enough, she would have created enough friction for you to finally decide to put a stop to her."

Henrietta believed Mrs. Sheffield had planned on doing precisely that. Why hadn't Evie sensed it? "Why do you feel that way and why didn't I see it?"

Caro smiled. "Oh, that's because you are too trusting and always try to see the good side in people. The same can't be said about me."

"Really?"

Caro nodded. "In case you are wondering, you should never change that particular trait in your character."

"But shouldn't I, at least, try to become more observant and aware of the underlying threat some people pose?" Evie asked.

This time, Caro laughed. "Oh, there's no need for that, milady. You are surrounded by people who care enough to look after your interests. I'm sure Tom would have eventually warned you about Mrs. Sheffield."

Yes, but would she have listened?

Evie considered organizing an outing to the village but she suspected people would clam up around her.

Looking at Millicent, she wondered if she should impose on her adventurous spirit again.

Millicent's eyes brightened. "I am at your service, milady."

"I haven't said anything, Millicent."

Glancing at Caro, Millicent said, "You have this look that comes before you ask someone to do something. Anyone else wouldn't think twice before asking their maid to perform a task, but you…" Millicent shrugged. "You almost look apologetic."

"I think Millicent is trying to say you are too considerate and sensitive of other people's feelings."

"Oh, I'm not sure if I should take that as a compliment or not. Doesn't it leave me wide open? People will think I'm weak."

"I believe the dowager would tell you not to concern yourself with what other people think." Caro looked up at the ceiling for a moment and then added, "And in the same breath, she would commend you for upholding a sense of decorum."

Evie clasped her hands together and leaned forward. "Millicent, would you mind returning to the village to find out what you can about Miss Anna Weston?"

Millicent smiled from ear to ear. "It would be my pleasure, milady."

Something had triggered the woman's outburst. Anna Weston had felt strongly enough to act on her feelings. Had Mrs. Sheffield resided in the county long enough to form a close friendship with Anna Weston?

If Anna Weston felt she had lost a true friend, she would have reason to feel embittered. If they had been true friends, even for a short time, had Mrs. Sheffield confided in her? And if she had, what had she said?

What if Mrs. Sheffield had concocted some sort of fictional backstory to justify her remarks about Evie?

So much for always seeing the best in people…

"Millicent, do you think you might be able to befriend Anna Weston?"

Millicent looked quite pleased with herself when she said, "I will not rest until I know everything there is to know about her."

Chapter Fourteen

As she descended the stairs, Evie peered down and murmured, "Not a creature was stirring, not even a mouse." She had been taught to enter a room with confidence, but a sense of trepidation swept through her. What would she find on the other side of the door?

Talk of murder and mayhem?

She reached the bottom of the stairs but did not move. Normally, she swept across the hall and straight into whichever room she needed to go to without a second thought.

A footman emerged from the dining room. Seeing her, he bowed his head and stepped aside.

Evie knew she had to move. Producing a smile, she squared her shoulders, and put one foot forward and then the other.

She could hear the flow of murmured conversations wafting toward her from the dining room. When she reached the door, she again hesitated but Henrietta had already spotted her.

"There you are, Evangeline. I had begun to worry about you."

"My apologies, Henrietta. I couldn't decide which dress to wear." A footman drew out a chair for her. She settled down and glanced around the table. "I hope you have all had a fruitful morning. I feel I should apologize. There have been so many disruptions, I can barely hear myself think. I can't imagine how you are all managing. I promise you, these are unusual circumstances…"

Zelma gave her a bright smile. "There is no need to apologize, my lady. In fact, we are almost overwhelmed by the amount of stimulation. Our heads are buzzing with so many ideas, we can barely keep up with them."

"I'm so glad to hear that." Well, not really, Evie thought and wondered if the scriptwriters expected her to continue supplying them with chaos.

The less informal sitting arrangements during lunch meant Evie could sit next to Henrietta.

"Zelma did not exaggerate," Henrietta murmured. "I watched them for nearly an hour and felt dazzled by the energy and enthusiasm. Oh, before I forget. I hope you realize you will have to invite the vicar to dinner."

"Thank you for the reminder, Henrietta. I might actually delay issuing an invitation."

"Oh? I would have thought you'd want to invite him as soon as possible in order to extricate all the information you can from him. He must know something. Everyone in the county will have made an effort to introduce themselves, and you know what that means. They will all have discussed recent events."

"Yes, I suppose you're right." Evie looked up and noticed Edgar standing nearby. "I wonder how Edgar is coping. It must be odd to be asked to join the group and then be excluded from it."

"I see. You wish to change the subject. Edgar is quite content with the circumstances," Henrietta assured her. "After this morning's session, he said he needed to devote some time to his duties for fear the others might resent him. I sat close enough to him to also hear him murmur something about being at risk of getting too big for his boots."

"That's just silly, but I suppose he knows best." Evie took a moment to admire the dainty little pork pie on her plate. She knew the pastry would be buttery and the filling just as delectable. "How is the play progressing?"

"If you ask me, I think they are short of suspects," Henrietta remarked. "So far, they have only managed to involve everyone living in the house."

"Where did the murder in the play take place?"

"In the village."

"Did anyone leave the house at the time?"

"Yes, we all did, at one point or other and our alibis are quite flimsy, including yours, my dear. Any one of us could be the poisoner." Henrietta leaned forward to include Tom in the conversation. "Tom suggested you would make the perfect poisoner."

"He did?" Evie turned to her right and glanced at Tom.

"Well, I had to distract them and the only way I knew how was to pretend to contribute something," he said. "Those women can be quite tenacious and haven't given up trying to talk me into joining their play."

"You could just walk away," Evie suggested.

"Someone has to keep an eye on them."

Phillipa laughed at something Zelma Collins said and

then turned to Evie. "We loved hearing the story about the vicar. So much so, Zelma thought it would be fun to include a character based on him in the play. I think you'll like what she has come up with."

"I'm almost afraid to ask." And she couldn't even begin to imagine what they would do with a newly arrived vicar. She considered sharing the information Millicent had passed on to her, but then she decided Henrietta didn't need to know the villagers thought she had been possessed.

"We have made the vicar a possible suspect," Phillipa continued. "So far, we have decided that our fictional Mrs. Sheffield had, until recently, lived in London where she had become acquainted with the vicar, who'd also resided in town. A scandal has driven him to the countryside and Mrs. Sheffield is the only one who knows about his past. We think that gives him a perfect motive to kill her."

Henrietta leaned in and whispered, "If only that could be true. Then the vicar would be sent away and we could get a new one."

"Henrietta! Don't you like our new vicar?"

Henrietta's eyes sparkled with mischief. "There is something odd about him. I feel I must agree with Tom. He is peculiar."

While Evie didn't necessarily wish to share the sentiment, she had sensed something strange about him too. Wouldn't someone in his position refrain from forming hasty opinions about someone? Yet, the vicar's reaction to Henrietta suggested he might have taken the villagers' gossip seriously.

Yes, Evie thought, he should have remained neutral.

"You look pleased with yourself," Tom said.

"I believe I have just had a personal breakthrough."

She mentioned Caro's remark about her tolerant character and went on to say she had just been quite critical of the vicar. At least, in her mind. "Also," she lowered her voice, "I must admit, I was dreading coming down for lunch. Yesterday, we had that dreadful incident with Anna Weston and then the police came…" Drawing in a deep breath, she finished by saying, "Perhaps we can now relax and enjoy an uneventful day, which should make the afternoon rehearsals something to look forward to." And she could fade into the background and play a game of Solitaire…

Henrietta murmured, "I would love to ask your cook to pass on the recipe for this wonderful pastry, Evangeline, but I'm afraid that will only cause friction in my household. My cook is rather sensitive and she will think I don't appreciate her pie. I do, but there is something to be said about an exceptional pie crust."

"I will make a point of inviting you to lunch when we have pie, Henrietta. That way, everyone will be happy."

"You are so thoughtful, my dear. How you could possibly have poisoned Mrs. Sheffield is anyone's guess. Of course, I am referring to your fictional character."

"Thank you for clarifying that, Henrietta."

Edgar cleared his throat and approached Evie.

"What is it, Edgar?"

"The detective, my lady. He wishes to speak with you."

Evie's voice hitched, "Now?"

"I'm afraid so, my lady."

"Only me?"

Edgar nodded.

"I'll come with you," Tom offered.

"Thank you but I can't help feeling he is being rather inconsiderate. Then again, it might be an emergency."

"Well, he hasn't asked to see me," Henrietta said. "I am happy to read that as a good sign."

As Evie made her way out of the dining room, she thought she heard Henrietta murmuring something about reality mimicking fiction.

Feeling slightly irritated by yet another interruption to lunch, Evie didn't give the remark much thought. However, as she was about to enter the library, she stopped.

"What?" Tom asked.

"I just added two and two together."

Tom grinned. "And what did you come up with?"

"Patsy Bolivar."

"Isn't that a character from a vaudeville skit?" Tom asked.

"Yes. I take it you know of him."

He nodded. "Whenever something goes wrong, blame Patsy Bolivar."

"In other words," Evie said, "Patsy was a fall guy."

"And?"

"My fictional family is pointing the finger of blame at me for poisoning the fictional Mrs. Sheffield and I suspect I'm about to be questioned by the detective about it."

"Oh, I see. Life imitating fiction."

Chapter Fifteen

When Evie walked into the library, the detective surged to his feet.

"Lady Woodridge, please accept my apologies for once again intruding on you."

"I take it this time you have some questions for me, detective." Evie considered remaining standing but then decided against it. After all, the detective had a job to do and it would be unkind to pressure him into getting on with it by making him feel uncomfortable.

While Evie chose to sit opposite him, Tom made his way to the fireplace.

"As a matter of fact, yes, I do have some questions. I wanted to ask you about the afternoon tea you held several days ago. The one Mrs. Sheffield attended."

So much had happened since that fateful day, Evie wondered if she would be able to remember any of it.

"How did Mrs. Sheffield look to you?" he asked.

Evie searched her mind. How could she describe a woman who had been so critical of her? She'd had an opinion about everything. Now that Evie thought about it, every time she'd glanced her way, Mrs. Sheffield had been talking with someone. Or, rather, she had talked in such a way, the other person hadn't been able to get a word in edgewise. Evie realized she had meandered off topic. The detective wanted to know how Mrs. Sheffield had looked…

"Sprightly." Evie tilted her head. "And chatty. She had a lot to say."

"So, she looked well?"

Had Mrs. Sheffield been unwell?

In Evie's mind, she'd looked lively and if she hadn't been well, then she might have been less… engaging.

"She'd looked well enough to me. Was there something wrong with her?"

"That's what we're trying to establish," the detective said.

"But you must know enough about her cause of death to feel you have to look into it," Evie reasoned. "I suppose you are not free to share any pertinent information."

The detective studied her for a long moment. Finally, he said, "I have been in contact with Detective Inspector O'Neill, my lady. He recommended sharing information with you."

Evie smiled. High praise indeed. However, Detective Inspector Jon Chambers did not look pleased about the idea.

Out of the corner of her eye, she saw Tom shifting. "Tom, how would you feel if the detective shared information with us?"

"I would be inclined to remind you of your desire to work in the garden," Tom drawled.

Meaning, she had been seeking any means possible to avoid the sort of circumstances which involved her in risky activities.

"I really don't see what possible harm it would cause," Evie mused.

"Right... well, in that case," the detective cleared his throat. "The dressmaker, Mrs. Green, described Mrs. Sheffield as looking pasty. Would you say Mrs. Sheffield looked off color during the afternoon tea party?"

"Are you trying to find out if the condition she succumbed to was actually present days before she died?" Evie thought that must be the case, otherwise, he would have requested to speak with Henrietta who had been present during Mrs. Sheffield's final moments.

"Yes."

Evie gave a slow shake of her head. "No, she didn't look unwell. I now realize this is something I noticed at the time. Her cheeks were colored. If I had to form an opinion about it, I'd say she'd been excited by the gathering and meeting new people." As she spoke, Evie tried to think what else might cause a person's cheeks to color.

"Can you recall what Mrs. Sheffield ate?" the detective asked.

"I believe she enjoyed some fruitcake, but I can't be sure. You must understand, there were several people present that day."

"I assume you served tea."

Evie nodded. Sitting back, she remembered Mrs. Sheffield studying Evie's tea service. "Do you wish to know the blend of tea we use?" Evie stifled a gasp. Not long ago, the beverage she had served at an afternoon tea had come under suspicion.

"Actually, I wondered if Mrs. Sheffield made any specific requests for something she alone might have consumed."

Evie gave it some thought. "No. If she had, I would have complied."

When he gave his eyebrow a slight lift, Evie added, "At the risk of sounding too sensitive, she came across as being the type of person who would take exception to not getting her way. Had she asked for fresh goat's milk, I believe I would have sent someone out to find a goat and milk it right in front of her."

The detective got up. "Thank you for your time, my lady."

Surprised by the brevity of his visit, Evie rose to her feet. "My pleasure, detective. I'm only too happy to assist." But, had she? Evie watched the detective leave and then turned to Tom. "At the risk of sounding like the dowager, what just happened?"

Tom brushed his fingers across his chin. "I'm not sure."

Evie tapped her foot. "For a moment there, I thought he might divulge some pertinent information."

Tom agreed. "Yes, I expected that too."

"I think he tricked me."

Tom nodded. "He provided you with a false sense of self-worth and made you believe he would confide in you."

"I wonder…" Evie tapped her chin.

∼

Half an hour later, Tom steered the motor car along the

road leading to the village and asked, "Are you still wondering? You issued instructions to get the car ready but you failed to share your thoughts."

"The detective didn't say how Mrs. Sheffield died but he showed interest in how she had looked days before she died. I'm thinking they are still trying to work out a cause of death and are, quite possibly, considering something that…" Evie shook her head. "No, I can't put my finger on it."

Tom said, "If it helps, I do believe you are on the right track. Either the detective thinks Mrs. Sheffield had a condition which led to her death or something she ate contributed to her death."

"Yes." Evie brightened. "Yes. That's it. He'd wanted to know if she had made any special requests. Now, we need to figure out what that something is. What sort of special request would she have made at an afternoon tea that might possibly… maybe bring about her death?"

"Something she might have been allergic to," Tom suggested.

Frowning, Evie said, "Some people are allergic to certain types of fish, but that's not something I would serve at an afternoon tea party. Oh… I served lobster sandwiches once but not on the day in question." Evie twiddled her thumbs. The detective had been quite underhanded. In the next breath, Evie argued with herself thinking the detective had merely used the necessary tactics to gain her co-operation. "He's up to something."

Tom glanced at her. "Sorry, I missed that."

The roadster hit a bump on the road. Evie's hand flew to her hat. "I'll tell you when we stop."

Tom slowed down for a farmhand making his way

across the road with his horse and cart. "Are you sure you want to do this?"

"I would prefer to avoid it but needs must. Besides, I believe we are expected. If you need to advice against it, now is the time."

He nodded. "I think visiting Mr. Sheffield is a bad idea."

"Is that all you have to say?"

"Admit it. This isn't just about paying your respects. You want to delve."

Evie lifted her chin. "You can blame the detective."

"How so?"

"He… taunted me into taking action and becoming involved."

"That's the part I don't quite understand."

Evie pushed out a breath. "You said it yourself. He led me to believe he would be sharing information with me and he didn't. He only dangled a carrot by suggesting Mrs. Sheffield had been suffering from some sort of malaise which had been exacerbated by something she ate or drank at my tea party."

"And now you feel it is your duty to fill in the gaps."

"The alternative," Evie said without sounding too defensive, "is to throw myself into gardening and we know how badly that turned out last time."

"I see there is no talking you out of it." With the road now cleared, Tom put the car into gear and drove the rest of the way into the village.

Evie pointed ahead. "The Sheffield house is two rows away from the vicarage."

"So the land Mrs. Sheffield inherited is not attached to the house," Tom mused.

"I guess not. That's not unusual." The house came into view. It appeared to have a sizable garden around it with mature fruit trees and a few ornamental ones. Tom parked the motor car outside the iron gates.

A woman dressed in black emerged from the house. Walking past them, she glanced at Evie and, recognizing her, she smiled and hurried away.

"How long do you think it will be before news about your visit spreads?" Tom asked.

"Half the village will have heard about it by now. I hope Millicent is still hovering around the village. It will be interesting to know how much information that woman will pass on."

A butler dressed in black welcomed them and led them through to a lovely drawing room perfectly situated to receive the afternoon sunshine.

"The Countess of Woodridge and Mr. Tom Winchester," the butler announced.

Mr. Sheffield approached them and extended his hand. Offering her condolences, Evie apologized for the intrusion.

"We are glad of company, my lady," Mr. Sheffield said and introduced his sister and his sister-in-law.

Elizabeth Sheffield gave her a warm smile. "How very kind of you to call on us, my lady. It is unusual for a house in mourning to open their doors to visitors," Elizabeth Sheffield said, "But my brother and I felt Miriam would want it this way."

Miriam?

Charlotte Davis, Mrs. Sheffield's sister, gave a small nod. "Yes, my sister would have found the company comforting. Miriam always enjoyed good company." Reed thin, the woman wore severe black and clutched a handkerchief in her hands. She looked to be about Evie's age. Perhaps older.

Miriam. Understanding dawned. Somehow, Evie had difficulty thinking of Mrs. Sheffield as Miriam. The name sounded too gentle for someone with such a determined character.

The butler appeared with a fresh pot of tea. In no time, they were settled around the fireplace drinking tea and scrutinizing each other. When no one spoke, Evie wondered if they were waiting to take their prompt from her.

As often happened, some people felt compelled to become reserved when in the company of someone with a title.

This left Evie with the arduous task of leading the conversation. She also needed to decide if she should be tactful and avoid asking any indelicate questions...

Before she could decide how to proceed, Mr. Sheffield cleared his throat.

He spoke in a calm tone, "The service is set for this coming Sunday. My daughters are making their way as we speak."

Mrs. Sheffield's sister, Charlotte Davis, huffed. "One would think they would want to be here and help you in your hour of need. Their mother would have had something to say about that. They only think of themselves."

It seemed Charlotte Davis shared a common trait with her sister.

"The girls will be here as soon as they can make the necessary arrangements," Elizabeth Sheffield said, her voice heavy with grief. "You know they have households to run and cannot abandon everything at a moment's notice."

"Still… It seems rather callous of them," Charlotte Davis continued.

Evie didn't dare look at Tom for fear they might both give away their surprise at such a conversation.

Charlotte Davis turned to Evie. Smiling, she offered her some lemon cake.

"It looks delectable. Thank you."

"It was very gracious of you to invite Mrs. Sheffield to afternoon tea, my lady," Mr. Sheffield said. "She spoke very highly of you." His gaze dropped to the table with the tea service and he sighed.

When his sister and sister-in-law followed suit, Evie glanced at the table. She didn't see anything unusual.

A teapot. Teacups. A plate of fruitcake. The lemon cake Evie had been offered. Strangely, the fruitcake remained untouched.

As she looked away, she noticed something else.

A pot of honey.

She hadn't seen anyone helping themselves to honey. Her granny always made sure to start the day with a spoonful of honey to ward off whatever might decide to attack her. She swore by it. Then again, she also swore by the glass of medicinal whisky she enjoyed every evening…

Evie leaned slightly forward. Yes, it was definitely honey. Noticing she had drawn everyone's attention, she said, "It's a pretty tea service."

"My sister's favorite," Charlotte Davis said. "And, of course, the honey she loved so much. I understand you keep your own hives, my lady."

Mr. Sheffield chortled. "Of course, Halton House took a ribbon last year."

"Oh, I didn't know you had been living in the district that long." In fact, Evie had been under the impression the Sheffield family had only recently re-settled in the area.

"We had tenants while we lived in town and I had a farm manager taking care of everything else. The tenants and the manager kept me abreast of all the goings on in the village."

So, Mr. Sheffield had taken care of business. It made Evie wonder if he had land holdings of his own. "And are you from the area too, Mr. Sheffield?"

"Next county up. Wiltshire. Elizabeth and I still have family there."

As Elizabeth Sheffield poured herself another cup of tea, Evie watched to see if she would use some of the honey to sweeten her drink.

She didn't.

Her attention remained fixated on the ceremonial pot of honey. Of all the things that might have been used to commemorate Mrs. Sheffield's absence, why honey?

Sitting back, she met Mr. Sheffield's gaze.

He smiled and asked, "Are you entering your honey in this year's fair, my lady?"

"Yes, I believe we are."

He tapped his nose. "I think we might give you a run for your money this year. My beekeeper has been taking particularly good care of our bees."

Elizabeth Sheffield sighed. "A blue ribbon for the best honey. Miriam would have loved that."

Evie looked up from her teacup in time to catch Charlotte Davis grimacing. In disapproval?

Chapter Sixteen

"Folks are usually about as happy as they make their minds up to be."
– Abraham Lincoln

"What an odd family," Evie remarked as they drove away from Mrs. Sheffield's house. "Even as I make allowances for their state of grieving, I wouldn't be surprised to discover that is how they behave on any given day." Evie laughed under her breath. "Then again, who am I to talk? I'm quite used to the people in my life behaving oddly, but an outsider might perceive their behavior in a different light." Following a butterfly as it made its way across the road and headed toward the meadows beyond, she asked, "Did you notice anything of significance?"

Tom shook his head, only to then shrug. "I might be wrong, but I think the husband looked just fine."

"Are you suggesting he is not at all sorry his wife died?"

"As I said, I might be wrong."

"He is very proud of his honey." Evie tapped her finger against her chin. "Should we look into it? Remember, the detective alluded to something when he asked if Mrs. Sheffield had made any special requests at my afternoon tea party. He might have been thinking about honey."

"And why would honey have had anything to do with her death?" Tom asked.

"I'll have to think about it."

"Or, you could share the information with the scriptwriters," Tom suggested. "I'm sure they will be only too happy to assist."

"Yes, I have no doubt they'll want to help… By including the information in their play." Evie pointed to a lane up ahead. "Make a turn there. From memory, it will lead us to the beekeeper's cottage. He's one of the few estate workers I never quite got around to meeting. I feel he might be able to provide some answers for us."

Evie sat back to admire the pretty scenery unfolding before them. Rows of trees lined one side of the lane and they were all in flower. "Just follow the trees. I believe there will be a gate up ahead. The trees actually form a wall around the property."

Tom laughed. "That's one way to keep the bees happy and contained."

"Yes, I think that is the point." She looked into the distance and couldn't help thinking out loud, "I wonder if our bees mingle with other bees."

Tom brought the car to a stop and hopped out to open the gate.

Evie emerged from the car. "We'll walk the rest of the way. I wouldn't want to disturb the bees."

"They're probably too busy to notice us," Tom said.

"I'm thinking about the fumes from the motor car. Bees respond to smoke, so they might also react to fumes. I wouldn't want to annoy them. They are such industrious little creatures, they deserve our respect."

Tom held the gate open for her. As Evie walked on through, he said, "You have a bee in your bonnet."

"I suppose you think I have become obsessed with Mrs. Sheffield's death. Do I need to remind you the police have called on me not once but twice?"

"I meant to say you have a bee *on* your bonnet. Would you like me to shoo it away?"

"You said it was *in*… Oh, never mind. It will fly away, I'm sure." After a moment, Evie asked, "Is it still there?"

"It's circling around the flower on your hat. I guess it's not the brightest bee in the hive."

They followed the path which eventually led them to a small cottage with a tidy yard and a pretty display of ornamental shrubs.

Evie looked around. "I hope someone notices us. I'm afraid I have never been introduced to the beekeeper."

After a few minutes, they heard someone approaching from the rear of the cottage. A tall man with a bushy beard and a mop of wild hair greeted them.

"Good afternoon," Evie said. "I hope we haven't caught you at a bad time." She introduced herself and Tom.

"Milady. I'm Ned Fordham."

Evie smiled. "I cannot begin to tell you how much I enjoy your honey, Ned. It is exceptional."

"I have little to do with that, milady. The bees do all the work."

"And so they do." Pointing at the trees surrounding the property, she asked, "What sort of trees are they?"

"Apple trees, milady. They're buzzing with bees at this time of the year."

Evie wondered if that affected the flavor of the honey. "Ned, do they feed on anything else?"

"Our bees? No, milady. Of course, there are always a few strays who wander into the garden and settle on a flower, but they mostly want the apple blossoms."

"What about other beekeepers? Do they plant apple trees too?"

Ned brushed his hand along his beard. "There are several orchards in the area. I'm sure the local bees find their way to the trees, but we're the only ones in the district to plant the apple trees specifically for the bees." Ned smiled and lowered his voice. "Then, we also have our secret ingredient."

Evie's eyebrows curved up in surprise. "Is that what makes our honey taste so exceptionally good?"

He nodded.

"What's the secret ingredient? Or is it too much of a secret to share even with me?"

"Orange blossoms, milady."

"Oranges? Isn't it too cold here for orange trees?"

"Ordinarily, yes, milady. However, we have been nurturing orange trees for well over 300 years." He nudged his head toward the rear of the property. "We have a large greenhouse and the trees are grown in tubs, which I bring out in the springtime."

"Fascinating. I can't remember honey tasting so good.

I believe we will take out another ribbon at the fair this year."

Ned grinned again.

Reading the expression, Evie said, "Ned, I think you have another secret weapon up your sleeve."

"I do, milady. Last year, we introduced kumquats. Would you like to see the hives?"

"Oh, perhaps another time, Ned. I'm afraid we must be getting back and I really don't wish to disturb the bees." She turned to leave only to stop. "Actually, do you know anything about Mr. Sheffield's bees?"

"Mr. Sheffield from the Davis farm?"

"Yes."

"I can't say that I do, milady. But then, I don't really get out and about. I don't like to leave the hives alone for any length of time."

"That's very commendable, Ned. Thank you for your time." Turning to Tom, she asked, "Is the bee still in my bonnet?"

∼

"I wish I'd thought of something else to ask Ned," Evie said as they made their way back to Halton House.

"That's assuming we're on the right track," Tom said.

"Well, nothing else springs to mind. My reasoning tells me honey might have something to do with Mrs. Sheffield's death, and I reached that conclusion because she seemed to have a penchant for it."

"That's all well and good," Tom argued, "but how exactly will it tie in with her death? And what if she died of natural causes?"

Evie gave it some thought and then said, "The police must have their suspicions otherwise they would cease their investigation. Oh… I do wish I'd brought up the subject of the police when we visited Mr. Sheffield but I had been too sensitive of his grief. Mr. Sheffield might have let something slip. According to the detective, the family asked the police to look into Mrs. Sheffield's death. Mr. Sheffield must surely have some sort of suspicions. Otherwise, why would he insist the police become involved? Now I'll have to think of another excuse to visit him."

"Or you could wait until the funeral service."

"True, but that's not until Sunday. I would prefer this unpleasant business be wrapped up by then."

"Well, if you think about it," Tom said, "Mrs. Sheffield hadn't lived in the district long enough to attract enemies. Oh, wait… I forgot about you."

"Tom, how could you? Surely, not even in jest. Although, you do have a point. If Mrs. Sheffield died under suspicious circumstances, then someone must have wanted her dead."

"I nominate her sister-in-law."

"Really? Elizabeth Sheffield? On what grounds? Her grief appeared to be genuine and profound."

Tom tapped his finger on the steering wheel. "We know enough about Mrs. Sheffield to believe she could not have been the easiest woman to live with. What if she made Mr. Sheffield's life miserable?"

"You actually think Elizabeth Sheffield would take matters into her own hands to liberate her brother from an oppressive wife? She'd have to be quite cold-blooded."

"What exactly is your point?" he asked.

"She didn't strike me as being cold-blooded. On the contrary. She seemed to be quite sensitive."

"That can be faked," Tom reasoned.

Yes, appearances could be deceptive. "I'm not prepared to form opinions just yet. Remember, they are in mourning. People don't always react the way one expects them to. I tried to soldier on, but in the end—" Evie broke off. She didn't like talking about her loss. Sighing, she removed her hat and inspected it.

"Are you making sure you don't have a stowaway?"

She smiled at him. "Bee in my bonnet, indeed."

As they approached the Halton House gatehouse, Evie found herself thinking about bees and blossoms. "Here's something else I wish had occurred to me." She tapped her hat. "I wonder if there are any flowers bees should stay away from." They had recently learned about plants which could be poisonous to animals. So, there might be certain flowers bees needed to keep away from...

Tom brought the car to a stop and turned to her. "We could go back to the apiary tomorrow and ask Ned or... We could spend some time in the library researching it. I can't think of a better way to avoid the scriptwriters. They are determined to give me a role in their play."

"You seem to forget the scriptwriters are working in the library."

"No, they're not. I heard them say they wanted a change of scenery and would be working in the pink drawing room."

"In that case, doing research in the library sounds like a solid plan. I'll join you shortly." Evie excused herself saying she wanted to check in on the scriptwriters.

Easing the door to the drawing room open, she looked up in time to see Henrietta rushing toward her.

"Evangeline. You cannot be here right now. You're not in this scene and we're all talking about you. It would be quite awkward for you to be present."

"W-why?"

Henrietta looked over her shoulder and lowered her voice. "You'll make Edgar nervous and uncomfortable."

"Surely not. He is accustomed to having me around."

"This is different. If you must know, *Lord* Edgar rescued you from the poorhouse. Now you've killed Mrs. Sheffield. We are trying to decide your fate and if you insist on being here, I'm afraid Edgar will feel obligated to go easy on you."

"Heavens, and we can't have that."

"No, we can't."

Moments later, Evie walked into the library, her lips slightly parted.

Tom laughed. "What news do you bring from the drawing room?"

"At some point, that will cease to be humorous. You won't believe this. I have been asked to keep out of the drawing room because I might disrupt the flow of creativity and lessen the harsh punishment they feel I deserve. I would ring for some tea but I'm afraid of disrupting the footmen who are no doubt standing by the other door to the drawing room with their ears pressed against it."

Tom drew a book out from the shelf and studied it. "Are you about to say you have become superfluous in your own house?"

Glowering at the library door, Evie said, "I feel I should storm in there and plead my case."

Tom handed her a book. "Put your mind to good use."

"Oh, I see we do have books on bees. Why am I surprised? We seem to have books on every subject under the sun." Evie settled down to read but she didn't get beyond the title page.

The door to the library opened and Caro and Millicent stepped inside.

"Is this a good moment, milady?" Caro asked.

"Come in. Come in. Dare I ask? What news do you bring?" She gestured for them to sit. As expected, both Caro and Millicent hesitated. "Oh, please do sit down."

They both obliged and sat on the edge of their seats.

"Mission accomplished, milady," Millicent declared. "I have befriended Miss Anna Weston."

"Oh, that was fast work." Evie waited for Millicent to reveal more but her maid's attention had drifted to Tom. "Millicent, you remember Tom."

Millicent grinned and nodded.

Tom looked up from his book. "Hello, Millicent."

Millicent responded by fluttering her eyelashes and giggling.

Heaven help us all, Evie thought. She gave the young maid a moment to recover and then, clearing her throat, Evie asked, "Did you find out anything else?"

Shifting in her seat, Millicent finally managed to tear her eyes away from Tom. "Yes, milady. Anna Weston is full of anger and resentment. Mrs. Sheffield had promised to introduce her to a suitable man. And now she's dead."

"Really? Anna Weston wants to marry?"

Millicent nodded. "She mentioned several prospects

slipping through her fingers over the years. I must say, at one point, I felt scared. She appeared to fixate on how her life should have been and blamed several locals for ruining her chances."

"That's not a good sign," Caro murmured.

Evie felt compelled to agree. Not everyone had the ability to accept responsibility for their actions or their lives. "Yes, but at least it puts Anna Weston in the clear. Surely, she would not have harmed someone who had offered to help her."

"Oh, does that mean Mrs. Sheffield was murdered?" Caro asked.

"No. I'm sorry, I didn't mean to mislead you or stoke the fires of suspicion." Turning back to Millicent, Evie asked, "How exactly did you befriend Anna Weston?"

"I strolled by her cottage a couple of times and finally caught her attention. She had been tending to her garden. When she invited me in, she led me through to the rear garden where she had set up a table for afternoon tea. I asked if she'd been expecting someone because there were two teacups. That's when she told me she had become accustomed to Mrs. Sheffield dropping in."

"Did she happen to have a pot of honey?" Evie asked.

"Oh, yes. It was one of those earthenware brown pots with honey written on it. When I tried to help myself to some, she moved the pot away from my reach saying the pot was empty. I'm not sure I believed her. That's when I had the feeling I should run for my life. She had this odd look about her. She stared at me without blinking. Of course, if you wish me to, I will return, but I can't say I'll be happy about it."

Evie gave her a reassuring smile. "I wouldn't ask you

to do something that puts you in danger." If she hadn't been convinced before, Evie now believed she had reason to question Miss Anna Weston's emotional stability. "Did she mention anything about attending the service?"

Millicent nodded. "She said she would be preparing a special bouquet."

Evie patted the book she still held. "Tom, it appears we might be on the right track after all." Honey seemed to be a key element in this mystery.

"There's something else, milady. Anna Weston doesn't seem to like you very much."

"Did she say why?"

"Well, when Mrs. Sheffield received an invitation to attend Mrs. Ellington's farewell afternoon tea, she suddenly had no time for Anna Weston. If you ask me, I'd say the woman had been biding her time until the local gentry accepted her into their inner circle. Anyhow, Anna Weston holds you responsible for breaking up her friendship with Mrs. Sheffield."

Evie heard Tom put his book down.

"What do you make of that, Tom?" Evie asked.

"Anna Weston finds a new friend who promises to change her life by introducing her to a suitable man and then the woman abandons her." Tom shrugged. "I'd say Miss Anna Weston has conflicting reasons to feel resentful."

Evie would have to agree, but how far would Anna Weston go and what measures would she have at her disposal? That led Evie to entertain a stray thought. While she and Tom needed to refer to books, Evie knew there were people around who held the information they sought at their fingertips. Did Anna Weston know anything about honey? Did she know about Mr. Sheffield's apiary?

"Millicent, do you know if Anna Weston ever met Mrs. Sheffield's family?"

"She didn't. I know that with absolute certainty because she made a point of telling me Mrs. Sheffield had found one excuse after the other to avoid inviting her to her house. So, Anna Weston went from politely inviting me to afternoon tea, to ranting about all her grievances. Including the ones she holds against you. Did I mention she doesn't like you very much?"

Tom chortled.

Evie slanted her gaze toward Tom. "I find your amusement out of place."

"My apologies. I couldn't help myself," Tom said.

"What exactly did you find amusing?" Evie held up a hand. "I believe I know. You think I'm torn."

He smiled.

"In fact, you think I am torn between feeling sorry for Anna Weston and wanting to cast aspersions on her character."

He agreed with a smile. "And now, you're about to tell me Anna Weston is probably still in shock over her friend's death and so she cannot be held responsible for her fluctuating emotions."

"Grief is a difficult emotion to deal with. You find yourself needing to move on but you're unable to. It's a tug of war few of us are equipped to deal with." Straightening, Evie noticed Caro giving Millicent a nudge with her elbow. It was enough to distract her.

Had her odd relationship with Tom given rise to widespread speculation among her household staff?

"Did you part ways on good terms?" she asked Millicent.

"Oh, yes. In the end, that is, when I suddenly surged to my feet and made an excuse to leave, Anna Weston smiled brightly and invited me to return."

"You did very well, Millicent. Thank you."

Caro stood up. "Well, if you'll excuse me. I must return to the drawing room. We are in the midst of deciding what to do with you… milady."

Chapter Seventeen

"If you want to be happy, set a goal that commands your thoughts, liberates your energy, and inspires your hopes."
– Andrew Carnegie

Unable to sleep, Evie made her way down to the library. The evening had progressed smoothly with all dinner conversation revolving around the weather and country pursuits. It had struck Evie as odd until Phillipa had explained they were all taking a break from discussing the play. Of course, Evie understood they were merely trying to avoid discussing her fate, or rather, the fate of her fictional character.

She had almost felt compelled to raise the issue and argue in favor of her character but it seemed their minds had already been made up.

Evie considered going down to the kitchen to prepare herself a cup of hot chocolate but then she remembered the last time she had attempted to prepare herself a drink. Mrs. Horace had caught her red-handed and had sent her away saying she would prepare the drink for her, never mind that it had been well after midnight.

The mantle clock chimed the hour. It seemed too late to wake anyone up just because she had a craving for hot chocolate.

Something had stirred her awake. She and Tom had poured through several books before and after dinner but nothing had sprung out at them.

She settled in the library to read yet another book about bees. After absorbing more basic facts than she would ever need, she couldn't help wondering why humans were always compelled to domesticate creatures. Of course, it made sense to try to meet demands and control productivity…

Her thoughts jumped from domesticating bees to domesticating people. She didn't need to exert herself too much. Mrs. Sheffield's need to exercise her control over people had been clear from the start. She had tried to manipulate her. Had she also exercised her will over others? Had Anna Weston been held hostage by Mrs. Sheffield's influence?

What could Mrs. Sheffield possibly have gained from that activity? Delight at having her own way with people? At commanding them? Had Mrs. Sheffield thought of herself as a queen bee?

Tom had been right in thinking Mr. Sheffield had not looked as grief stricken as one might have expected him to be. However, Evie insisted people had their own individual way of dealing with grief.

For all they knew, he might still be lingering in denial, hence the need to involve the police in an investigation.

She wished the detective had been more forthcoming with information. "It would save everyone so much trouble," Evie murmured. And she wouldn't have to do so much reading...

As she turned the pages looking for a relevant chapter, Evie came across a folded piece of paper. She strained to read the scratchy scrawl. The note made reference to the benefits of introducing orange trees to the bees. Skimming through the chapter, Evie smiled. The piece of paper had been slipped into the relevant chapter. Someone had done their homework.

Deciding she had done enough reading for one night, she put the book away only to notice another title of interest. She drew the book out and took it back to her room.

After reading a couple of chapters on the history of honey, she turned the page and began reading about something called *mad honey*.

It sounded intriguing but then, the lines began to blur, so she set the book down and made herself comfortable for the night. That included counting her blessings.

As she did, she wondered if Mrs. Sheffield had counted her blessings or if she had made lists of people she had wanted to fix.

What had made her want to meddle in people's lives? Had she been unhappy with her lot?

Even without the privileges she enjoyed, Evie knew she could find something to be happy about. The sun warming her skin. The fresh air she breathed. Spring blooms. The fact she had eyes to see the beauty around her.

With that thought lingering in her mind, she forgot all about Mrs. Sheffield and drifted off to sleep.

∽

Rising early the next morning, Evie dressed herself and took her beekeeping book down to breakfast with her.

"Good morning, Edgar." Her butler inclined his head. "Am I the first to come down?" she asked as she helped herself to some eggs and toast.

"Yes, my lady."

Half an hour later, she still sat alone.

"More coffee, my lady?"

"Thank you, Edgar. I can't help wondering where everyone else is."

"They are in the library, my lady. The scriptwriters had an early start to the day and decided to have coffee there while they worked on the third act."

"Oh... how industrious of them."

The door opened and Tom strode in. "Ah, good. I see I'm in time for breakfast."

As he sat down with a plate full of sausages and eggs, he glanced at Evie's book. "Have you discovered anything new?"

"I read something interesting last night and thought I would browse through the chapter this morning to refresh my memory but..." she had been distracted by the fact she'd been alone.

She opened the book and flipped through the pages. "I recall reading something about crazy honey... No, not crazy. *Mad honey*. Yes, that's it. There's a part which describes the poisoning of Roman troops in the first century. They were marching to battle when they came across some honey. After eating it, they became confused and sick."

"Did they win the battle?" Tom asked.

"I assume they didn't. Sorry, I drifted off to sleep. Did you get anywhere with your research? I saw you take a book with you."

"I believe I am now well versed in the history of beekeeping." He looked at her book again. "That mad honey you mentioned sounds interesting."

"I'd like to visit Mr. Sheffield's hives today. I thought I might read more along the way."

"Where is everyone?" Tom asked.

"They're busy writing the third act."

"Oh, yes. That's the one where you take action and poison poor Mrs. Sheffield."

"It's actually Mrs. Hatfield and I suspect the scriptwriters might be trying to avoid me." Evie glanced at Edgar. "They decided my fate yesterday and today they probably can't face me."

Edgar looked away.

"I'll either be disowned by my family and end up back in the poorhouse or the lunatic asylum. Or worse. In prison. Is that worse or just as bad? Either way, my fictional family appear to be intent on disowning me."

They both looked at Edgar.

Tom laughed. "No, he's not giving anything away."

Edgar cleared his throat and lifted his chin. "With all due respect, my lady, it is not my place to do so."

"I'll take that as an admission." Evie turned her attention to the chapter about mad honey. "I should like to have a word with the detective and tell him about our findings. I think he will find it most interesting." When she looked up, she saw Tom and Edgar exchange a look of surprise. "You don't seem to agree."

"Don't concern yourself with my opinions," Tom said. "I rarely make any sense before I've had my second cup of coffee."

"Well, hurry up. I need a reliable sounding board. I still believe the detective wanted to bait me into snooping around. Remember, he showed an interest in how Mrs. Sheffield looked on the day of the afternoon tea party." Evie looked up and tried to remember what else had prompted her to take an interest. "Oh, and he also asked if she had made any special requests. I believe that is key to our current preoccupation."

"And you hope to impress him with a story about mad honey?" Tom asked.

Evie grinned. "I believe I am being more cunning than that. I hope to bait him into giving us more information. If he shows an interest in the mad honey idea, it will mean there is actually some substance to the theory, which I have yet to formulate."

"The theory which will propose Mrs. Sheffield loved honey so much, her killer decided to use it against her?" Tom asked.

"Yes. Now, eat up. I wish to visit Mr. Sheffield's apiary this morning."

"And what do you hope to find at Mr. Sheffield's apiary?"

"I must admit, I am curious about the flowering trees he keeps. We now know what makes Halton honey taste so extraordinarily good, it will be interesting to see where Mr. Sheffield is going wrong."

"Will you share your beekeeper's secret with him?" Tom asked.

Evie glanced at Edgar. "No, I don't believe I will. It's not my place to do so."

Edgar gave a small nod of approval.

Evie finished her coffee and said, "I propose setting off early. I would like to return in time for luncheon." She crossed her fingers. "Let's hope it's not interrupted."

∽

"I see you are still not taking any chances with your suits," Evie observed as they drove along a country lane leading to Mr. Sheffield's apiary. "Is my granny likely to arrive earlier than even you expect?"

"She sent a message saying she had sailed," Tom said. "I doubt she would go to the trouble of duping me just so she can make her arrival a real surprise."

Evie brushed her hand along her skirt. "I have made all the necessary arrangements but I do wish I'd been able to organize some new gowns. She is bound to notice."

"And will that be the end of the world?" Tom asked.

"Do I really need to remind you of the fact you have abandoned English tweed in favor of fashionable gray suits?"

Tom tipped his hat down.

"And where do all your suits come from? Honestly, I'm almost inclined to believe you really did strike it lucky in the oil fields."

Evie opened her bee book and turned her attention to discovering all she could about mad honey, including some of the symptoms. "Listen to this, mad honey can induce hallucinations." Heavens. After breakfast, she had returned to her room to change for their morning outing and she had told Caro she had stayed up late to read about honey. Millicent had been there helping Caro tidy up her room and she too had heard her talk about mad honey. Not that she'd known much about it then, but Millicent had said she would take care to avoid any type of honey...

By the time they arrived at Mr. Sheffield's apiary, Evie knew honey bees feeding off rhododendrons could produce mad honey. "I'll have to check with Ned Fordham to make sure we don't have any rhododendrons growing." Evie pressed her hand to her throat. "Heavens, what if we have been consuming mad honey?"

"It would certainly explain a great deal," Tom mused.

"Are you trying to suggest something?" Evie asked, her tone full of innocence. "I seem to recall you enjoying honey in the morning and being partial to Mrs. Horace's honey cake." Evie leaned forward. "Is that someone on a bicycle?"

"I need all the honey I can get just to keep up with your train of thought." Tom slowed down.

"Oh, she looks familiar."

As they approached the woman, she looked up and the bicycle wobbled slightly. That's when Evie thought the woman had recognized her. She reacted by leaning forward and putting more effort into her pedaling.

"Charlotte Davis," Evie said as they drove past her.

"Are you sure?"

Evie turned and watched the woman disappearing down the narrow country lane. "Yes." The day before, she'd worn mourning clothes, but now, she looked quite cheerful in a pretty floral dress. "Maybe she didn't recognize us."

Tom brought the car to a stop outside the gates to the apiary.

Climbing out of the roadster, Evie looked into the distance and saw Charlotte looking back over her shoulder. She hadn't acknowledged them. That could only mean she hadn't wanted to be seen…

Tom stood by the gate. "I suppose you want to be considerate toward the bees and walk the rest of the way."

"Yes, are you going to complain about it?"

"I wouldn't dare."

As they walked, Evie tried to identify the trees. They were mostly oak, maple and beech trees. They followed the path and found a cottage surrounded by a large plantation of trees in full flower.

The door to the cottage stood open. Moments later, a man appeared. He had mussed brown hair and looked slightly disheveled.

"Can I help you?" he asked.

Evie introduced herself. "And this is Mr. Tom Winchester."

The beekeeper nodded and introduced himself as "Benjamin Nelson."

"We wanted to ask you about your hives."

"They are not my hives, milady. They belong to the Sheffield family." He looked around him. "Although, this land used to belong to the Davis family."

The statement struck Evie as odd. Had Mrs. Sheffield surrendered ownership of her land to her husband? English law allowed married women to own and control property in their own right. A woman who enjoyed wielding her control would surely want to increase it…

"Have you lived here long?" Evie asked.

"Yes, all my life. My family has always looked after the bees."

Evie looked around and said, "I see you have apple trees."

"Yes, they're for the bees."

Noticing some other trees, she pointed at them. "What are those?"

"Cherry, milady. They flower early but continue on into April."

She couldn't see any orange trees in sight. "I hear Mrs. Sheffield was very fond of honey. I suppose you supply the Sheffield house."

"Of course. It's their honey."

Evie had wanted him to mention someone from the house had only just dropped by but he didn't say anything. "It's so pretty here. It would be lovely to have a picnic." She watched his reaction, but he gave nothing away. "I hear say Mr. Sheffield takes a personal interest."

"That he does, milady. He visits regularly. Did you want to try our honey, milady?"

"Oh, is that possible?"

He nodded and walked back inside the cottage. A moment later, he reappeared and handed her a small pot of honey.

"Out of curiosity, do you have rhododendrons planted here?"

He shook his head and pointed to the small garden in the front yard. "I have lavender and some other shrubs."

"Is there a reason for that?"

"We prefer the bees focus on the fruit trees and... rhododendrons are no good for bees. In fact, you don't want bees anywhere near rhododendrons, or azaleas."

"Really?" The fact he'd given them the information suggested he really didn't have anything to hide. Evie thanked him for his time and they left.

When they reached the roadster, Tom asked, "Did you get all the information you wanted this time?"

"No, not really. I couldn't bring myself to ask outright if Charlotte Davis had just visited him."

"You're too thoughtful for your own good," Tom murmured.

"Yes, I suppose... I think we should now head back to the village."

"Any particular reason?"

"Yes, I'm hoping we'll encounter Charlotte Davis along the way. I would bet just about anything she will deny riding out to the apiary."

"Do you think she wants to keep it a secret?"

"Absolutely. And before you ask why, I'll tell you. She wore a pretty dress." When Tom gave her a puzzled expression, she said, "She was in mourning yesterday, and today she's not."

Tom nodded. "Are you about to suggest she is somehow responsible for her sister's death?"

No, Evie thought. But... curiosity had taken a hold of her. "My mind is generating a few interesting notions." None she wished to share just yet. "There's an idea floating around my head." Had Charlotte Davis worn the pretty dress for the beekeeper? Instead of sharing the information with Tom, she changed the subject and said, "They have the same setup as we do, with someone living on the property and looking after the bees. I suppose that rules out the possibility of an outsider meddling with the hives."

"If someone did, they would have to know how to take the necessary precautions," Tom said.

Evie gave a distracted nod. Had Charlotte been to the apiary? If she had, why would she want to hide it? While she wanted to entertain the idea, she didn't feel entirely comfortable hatching a story about Charlotte and the beekeeper...

As Tom focused on his driving, Evie turned her attention back to her book. She read through the next chapter and, in her excitement, she flipped through the pages again looking for the key paragraph.

"Listen to this." She leaned in so Tom wouldn't miss anything. "The poisonous honey is commonly referred to as *mad honey*, a nickname earned because of the confusion it is known to cause. The toxin can cause very low blood pressure and heart rate as well as irregular heart rhythm. These symptoms could be life threatening."

"There you have it," Tom said. "One question remains. How does that information fit in with what... Well, I want to say what we know but we don't really know much. It would be a different story if the detective had at least told us how Mrs. Sheffield died. As it is, we can only speculate."

True.

As they neared the village, they saw Charlotte Davis riding along in her bicycle.

Tom slowed down and, when he caught up to Charlotte, Evie said, "Hello."

Charlotte's bicycle teetered and wobbled slightly.

Bringing her bicycle under control, she looked at them and gave them a tight smile.

"Would you like a lift back to the village?" Evie offered.

"No, thank you."

"Are you sure?"

Charlotte gave her a stiff nod.

"You must be tired from all that riding. The apiary is miles away."

"Oh, I'm fine. Thank you."

Interesting. She hadn't denied going to the apiary. "We've just been to visit the apiary."

Charlotte Davis couldn't pedal fast enough. She leaned forward and put all her effort into it.

Tom had no trouble keeping up with her.

She must have reached a point where she couldn't pedal any faster, so, instead, she came to a stop.

"Oh, do you need some help?" Evie asked.

"No. I'm fine. I just remembered I... I forgot something." She turned the bicycle around and pedaled away.

"That's one way to end a conversation," Tom said. "What now?"

Evie tried to decide. She supposed they could return to Halton House for lunch. "Except for the visit to Mr. Sheffield's house, we haven't been back in the village since the day Mrs. Sheffield died. I would like to walk around. Perhaps we might see or hear something of interest."

Chapter Eighteen

"If you want to gather honey, don't kick over the hive." - Dale Carnegie

*E*vie felt satisfied with their morning's adventure but she didn't wish to end it by returning to Halton House. "I'd say our chances of enjoying a quiet lunch are extremely good. The scriptwriters have been working since early this morning and I wouldn't be surprised if they have decided to work right through lunch. Regardless, I would like to play it safe. Let's enjoy lunch in the village. Do you have any suggestions?"

"Other than the pub?" Tom shrugged.

"The pub it is then."

"Are you sure?"

"Are you about to suggest the pub is not respectable enough for the Countess of Woodridge?"

"Not at all. After all, it has your family name on it."

When they entered, a few heads turned but Evie didn't see anyone straightening in their seats. If anyone had looked uncomfortable in her presence, she might have suggested going to the tearoom instead.

"I always expect to smell ale and yet I'm always surprised by the lovely aroma of something baking in the kitchen," she said.

Tom drew out a chair for Evie and settled down opposite her. Leaning in, he murmured, "the detective just entered."

Trying to be discreet, Evie glanced over her shoulder and saw the detective looking around the pub.

"Do you think he's looking for us?" Evie asked.

"If he wasn't before, he is now. He's heading this way."

The detective removed his hat and greeted them. "Lady Woodridge. Mr. Winchester."

"Detective. Would you care to join us?" Evie invited.

He didn't wait to be asked twice. "I must say, my lady, this is the last place I would have expected to find you."

"We have been out and about this morning," Evie explained. "It made sense to have lunch here. Were you looking for us, detective?"

He gave her what looked like an impish smile. "According to my colleague, Detective Inspector O'Neill, as soon as I gave you an update on my investigation you were most likely to start asking questions. I wonder if you have."

"As a matter of fact, yes. You piqued my curiosity." She watched his reaction but he gave nothing away.

"Would you care to share what you have discovered?"

Evie gave him a brisk smile. "Only if you share what you know about Mrs. Sheffield's death."

"That sounds like a fair exchange."

Evie's surprise was interrupted when the waitress came to take their orders. They all settled on the house specialty, pork pie.

Evie expected the detective to suggest she share some information first. Instead, he surprised her.

"Mrs. Sheffield had never been ill a day in her life," the detective informed them. "And then she suffered a heart attack." He drew out his notebook. "A myocardial infarction, to be precise."

Evie exchanged a knowing look with Tom. "And now you're looking at possible causes."

"Expert opinions vary. In the absence of a history of heart disease in the family, doctors look at the person's lifestyle."

"And what do the police look into?" Evie asked.

"If a doctor can't provide a reasonable explanation but suggest there might be something suspicious about the death, we start looking into motives for murder and possible suspects."

Evie brightened. The more she thought about it, the more she believed Mrs. Sheffield's need to manipulate people had landed her in trouble with someone.

"You seem cheered by the revelation, my lady."

"Oh, yes. Tom and I have been leading up to that discussion. While we haven't talked about motive or possible suspects, we have come across a possible weapon. Honey."

"Honey?"

Evie gave a vigorous nod.

The detective sat back and studied her. "And how did you come by that lead?"

"We stumbled upon it." Before the detective could ask for more information, she said, "I'm more interested in suspects. How do you come up with those?"

The detective thought about it for a moment and then said, "By retracing the victim's steps leading up to the final hours and by contacting the people she liaised with."

"I see. That's why you came to Halton House. Did a possible motive emerge from that meeting?" Evie answered her own question. "Of course not. Otherwise, I would have been taken into custody. Who else have you interviewed?"

The detective smiled. "Hasn't your maid informed you of my activities?"

Evie looked puzzled enough for the detective to explain that every time he'd emerged from somewhere, he'd spotted Evie's maid.

"Oh, you mean Millicent. How did you happen to know she works for me? Have you been spying on Halton House?"

Instead of answering her, the detective said, "Tell me about this theory involving honey."

Evie didn't care for the way he changed the subject and, in truth, she wasn't entirely comfortable with being spied on.

"I'm not sure I should. You might find the information I have to offer ludicrous."

"I promise to keep a straight face."

Tom laughed. And, while he didn't say anything, Evie imagined him thinking he had been trying to stop himself from laughing from the moment he had met Evie.

"Detective. Are you, by any chance, indulging me?"

"I wouldn't dream of it, my lady. Remember, I have been in contact with my colleague and he assured me you can be of great value, offering insightful observations."

"But you are not convinced of my value."

"Perhaps, but my reservations provide you with the opportunity to prove me wrong. You might even be able to have the last laugh at my expense."

"What do you think, Tom? Should we share our findings with the esteemed detective?" She sounded miffed and Evie had no doubt she also looked it.

Tom shrugged. "I think it's a solid idea. You might have to tell him or else risk being imprisoned for withholding valuable information."

"You're right. I do enjoy my freedom." She drew in a breath. "Mad honey…"

"I'm listening," the detective said.

"I believe I am about to share with you the most interesting part of our findings." Evie went on to explain the effects of this honey. "The toxin can cause irregular heart rhythm and the symptoms can be life threatening."

The detective brushed his hand across his chin. "And where does one obtain this honey from?"

She had no idea. None whatsoever. In fact, until she saw it with her own eyes, she would most likely believe it was nothing but a myth. "Anything can be purchased for a price. However, if you continue to focus on motive, you might find someone with the knowledge to acquire it. Where there is a will, there is always a way." She looked at Tom. "We just visited the Sheffield apiary and we met the beekeeper. We are not trained professionals so we… or rather, I couldn't think of anything significant to ask.

However, we talked about the flowers bees prefer. That's when the beekeeper mentioned rhododendrons. We decided that important bit of information would not be given freely by the killer. If, indeed, there is a killer."

When they were served their lunch, the conversation mellowed to pleasantries about the local village. Detective Inspector Jon Chambers had spent his entire life living in London. With the exception of a few family vacations to the seaside, he had never experienced life in a small village. Taking up a new posting in the nearby town of Reading had given him the opportunity to venture out and see more of the countryside.

"It's unsettling to hear there is actually need for a detective so close to our little village," Evie said.

The detective's eyebrow hitched up. "Do you believe fresh air makes you immune to crime?"

"No, of course not... I obviously need to deceive myself. Otherwise, I would never get any sleep." She considered asking for more detailed information about the rate of criminal activity in the area only to change her mind and decide she would prefer to remain blissfully ignorant. "Detective, did you question everyone at Mrs. Green's establishment?" After Henrietta's experience at the dressmakers, Evie hadn't been able to work up the courage to pay her a visit. She would eventually need to do something about that since Mrs. Green had been working on some gowns for her.

"I spoke with Mrs. Green, two maids and her new employee, Abigail Andrews."

"Oh, yes. The new assistant. She worked in Paris. I'm hoping she will be able to wave her magic wand over my gowns."

The detective tilted his head and looked at her without saying anything.

Evie glanced at Tom.

"I believe you have just piqued her ladyship's interest again," Tom murmured.

"I didn't say anything."

"No, but that was enough for the Countess."

The detective set his fork down. "How exactly did I do that?"

"By not commenting," Evie said. "Also, you didn't blink. I believe you have heard a different story about Abigail's background."

"Indeed, I have. Abigail Andrews told me she had recently worked in London."

Evie wished she had been there to hear it for herself. Had the assistant blushed? Had her voice sounded strained. Had she taken a deep swallow and wrung her hands together?

"Mrs. Green told me Abigail had worked in Paris," Evie said. "She might have been trying to secure my patronage by impressing me with Abigail's experience. Or, Mrs. Green might have been misinformed. People have been known to make extravagant statements about their experience, all in order to secure a position."

"You think Abigail Andrews lied?" the detective asked.

Why did he sound surprised? Surely, his line of work brought him face to face with people who lied all the time.

"How did she look to you when you asked her about her recent place of employment. In fact, when you spoke with her, did she seem on edge or was she happy to help you with your investigation?" Even as she asked the question, Evie made a note to visit Mrs. Green's establishment.

The dressmaker might not be happy to see her so soon after Mrs. Sheffield's death, but they still had some unfinished business. Evie had planned on visiting the following week for a dress fitting, but she saw no harm in bringing the date forward. It would be a perfect opportunity to meet her new assistant.

"Most people I interview are wary and rather nervous," the detective admitted.

"But some more than others," Evie said. "Would you say a guilty person is bound to slip up and give out information they were intentionally trying to withhold?"

"You take more than a haphazard interest in the law, my lady," the detective mused.

"I'm not sure what you mean, detective. However, I suspect you might be referring to my observation skills. They don't always work in my favor." Evie turned her attention to finishing her lunch, but she couldn't switch her thoughts off. "At which point do you decide you do not have any substantial leads to continue on with your investigation?" Evie smiled. "I think I might have answered my own question. Of course, if the people you interview fail to divulge anything suspicious, you would have no reason to pursue your investigation."

"I must admit, I had almost reached that point and then you mentioned the honey."

"Assuming someone used it as their weapon of choice, will you now try to find out how it was obtained?"

"Actually, this is where I need to convince my superiors there are reasonable grounds to continue putting in man hours."

"And if you fail?"

"I prefer to avoid thinking about that."

Evie noticed several people turning toward the door, including Tom.

Watching his expression, she tried to decide if it would be worth her while to see who had just entered the pub.

"It's the new vicar," Tom murmured. "And he just spotted you."

"Interesting," the detective said. "He was headed this way and, when he saw you, he changed direction. Why do you think that is?"

"I suppose you wish me to state the obvious. Our new vicar is trying to avoid me." Evie gave the detective a brief account of their first encounter. "I'm glad you find it amusing, detective."

With the meal finished, the detective checked his notebook. "As much as I have enjoyed our impromptu meal, I'm afraid I must now return to work."

When he left, Tom said, "I'm surprised you didn't share your observations about Charlotte Davis."

Evie feigned ignorance when she asked, "Which ones might they be?"

"You're suspicious of her. Clearly, she had been to the apiary but she didn't wish to admit it. She's hiding something."

"You can't expect me to jump to conclusions about everyone I meet. Perhaps she was just out and about, enjoying the lovely spring weather." Although, she had been quick to abandon her mourning clothes, and she hadn't looked pleased to encounter them.

What could she have been up to? Evie had recognized her from a distance, so Charlotte Davis had not been trying to disguise herself. Sitting back, Evie decided she didn't see anything wrong with a woman suffering from the loss of a sister going out for a ride in a country lane.

"You don't find it odd that she suddenly had to turn around?" Tom asked. "I think she wanted to avoid talking with you."

"Are you taunting me?"

"I believe I'm doing you a good turn. The more you involve yourself in Mrs. Sheffield's death, the less time you have to fret about your grandmother's visit."

"I suppose I should thank you. Now... Have we achieved enough today? Should we head back to Halton House?"

Standing up, she turned toward the door and noticed the vicar ducking his head as if trying to avoid making eye contact with her. "Well, this is going to be rather awkward. As the Countess of Woodridge, I will be sitting in the front pew at Sunday service and it is customary to stop and have a few words with the vicar at the end of the service. The man is acting in a such a way, I have a good mind to suspect him of hiding something."

Tom laughed. "Now all you need to do is connect him to Mrs. Sheffield and you have your killer." He held the door open and asked, "Are we heading back to Halton House or will you try your luck with Mrs. Green?"

"I am rather curious about Abigail." Evie stepped out of the pub and stopped. "Oh...Did the detective tell us who else he spoke with?"

"I don't believe he did."

He had mentioned retracing Mrs. Sheffield's last steps. That had led him to Halton House and to Mrs. Green's establishment. Had he also spoken with Mrs. Sheffield's sister and sister in law?

"Perhaps we should return to Halton House and present all our suspicions to the scriptwriters," Evie said. "I'm sure they will employ their imagination and come up with some interesting theories. I don't see any harm in making the best of the tools at our disposal."

Tom smiled at her. "Well, that's one way of diverting their attention away from making plain Evie Parker the family's scapegoat."

"Oh, but I believe my fate has already been sealed." When they reached the roadster, Evie stopped and looked across the street. "On second thought, I do think we should pay Mrs. Green a visit." Now or never, she thought.

Chapter Nineteen

"Are you sure you wish to visit Mrs. Green now?" Tom asked. "You don't really look that eager. I noticed your steps have slowed down and you're looking away."

"A moment ago, you were encouraging me," Evie mused. "If you must know, I'm trying to be casual and discreet. You know... Not so obvious. If we make a beeline for Mrs. Green's store, someone is bound to notice and exaggerate what they saw. I can just imagine what they'd say during their dinner table conversation." Evie deepened her voice. "The Countess was up to no good again, poking her nose where it doesn't belong, subjecting innocent people to her severe line of questioning."

The storefront had a couple of lovely dresses on display, something Evie thought would provide them with the perfect alibi.

"Let's pretend we're admiring them," she suggested.

"I'm not sure how I'm supposed to do that," Tom whispered.

"You could tilt your head as if in thought and... and point at something."

"And why exactly would I do that? In fact, why do you wish to delay entering the store?"

"There's a sign on the door. They appear to have stepped out to lunch. Who knows what 'back in five minutes' means. Five minutes, starting when?"

Evie strolled over to the next window. As she walked past the door, she tried to look through the lace curtain, but she didn't see anything. Taking a few moments to admire the next window, she then walked by the door again. When she leaned her hand on the doorknob, it opened.

"What are you doing?" Tom whispered.

"The door is open."

"Yes, I see that. You should close it now."

"But what if they have forgotten to lock up? It would be remiss of us to walk away now and leave the store unattended and vulnerable to burglars. In fact, I think I should go inside to make sure there are no burglars lurking about. If you'd prefer to wait outside..."

Tom pushed the door open, saying under his breath, "Someone was killed in there... maybe... we don't know yet. In any case, do you really think I would allow you to go in unaccompanied?"

They stepped inside and Evie eased the door closed.

"And why did you do that?" Tom asked. "Do you want to make sure the burglars don't escape?"

"I don't understand why you are being so critical. We are doing our civic duty."

"Strange. I always assumed that would involve contacting the local constabulary."

"They're busy hunting down a possible killer." Evie

ran her finger along the counter. There appeared to be a light layer of dust. "I think the store must have been closed after the incident."

Turning, her gaze settled on the far corner where a couple of chairs had been arranged between a small table with a teacup sitting on it.

Evie pointed at the table and chair and whispered, "Do you suppose that is where it happened?"

A noise coming from the back of the store had them both swinging around and then stilling.

Tom gestured toward the door. When Evie shook her head, he reached for her and pulled her toward the exit.

"Oh, Lady Woodridge."

"Mrs. Green." The dressmaker stood at the door to the back of the store wearing a beige smock and an apron over her dress. She looked slightly out of breath and clearly surprised to see them there.

"Were we expecting you today, my lady?"

Evie recovered from the surprise and said, "I don't believe you were, Mrs. Green, but I was telling Tom this morning we should stop by and ask if there is anything we could do for you."

Mrs. Green pressed her hand to her chest. "Heavens. I thought I might have forgotten an appointment."

"Oh, no, that's not until next week."

Mrs. Green visibly relaxed. However, her gaze went to the door.

"The wind must have pushed it open. We came in to make sure everything was fine." Evie signaled to the door. "The sign said you were out for five minutes."

"Yes, I'm afraid that is the only sign we have and we all left in such haste the other day, I didn't have time to change it. The police asked us to keep the store closed for a day while they looked around. Although, what they hoped to find, I have no idea. In any case, I decided to close the store for a few days. What with this dreadful business of Mrs. Sheffield..."

"Yes, we heard. I am so sorry that happened in your store. It must have been dreadful."

Mrs. Green nodded. "I sent the staff home. Although, you mustn't worry about your gowns, my lady. Abigail took them home with her and will be working day and night until she finishes them."

"That is highly commendable but I would understand if you are delayed." Evie looked around and tried to think of a way to delay their exit.

"My apologies, my lady. The place looks as though it has been derelict for years. I came in today to tidy up and I was just about to start in the front room. One of the windows was left slightly ajar and we tend to get a lot of dust from the street." Mrs. Green hurried to the small table and removed the teacup. "Is there something I can do for you today?" She looked around her and with no other place to set the teacup down, she put it back on the small table.

"Oh, no. We only wanted to make sure you were fine."

Mrs. Green nodded. "As you can see, I'm keeping myself busy. These last couple of days have only succeeded in reminding me I have no talent for leisure activities." Her hand pressed against her chest again and then dropped.

When she curled her fingers into the palm of her hand and then clutched both hands together, Evie began to feel responsible for Mrs. Green's fretting.

"I'm sorry. I really didn't mean to intrude. When do you think you'll open your establishment again?"

Mrs. Green took a visible swallow. "It's difficult to say, my lady. There have… there have been a couple of cancellations. It seems some of the ladies in the village are afraid."

Evie gasped. "Afraid of what?"

"Well, it's all nonsense if you ask me, but they seem to think the ghost of Mrs. Sheffield is lingering here."

"But… Why would they think that?"

"There is some sort of rumor going around. Some people are saying she died under mysterious circumstances."

"Heavens, who could have started those rumors?"

Mrs. Green pursed her lips. "I have no idea." Her voice hit a high note," But I can't help feeling someone means to harm my business." She wrung her hands together until her knuckles pushed against her skin. "I wish… I wish Mrs. Sheffield had found somewhere else to die."

Evie placed her hand on Mrs. Green's hand. "Don't you worry about that. Once you open up again, I will be your first customer and… and my grandmother is arriving soon. I will make sure she comes and orders an entire new wardrobe from you."

"That's very kind of you, my lady."

"We should leave you to it now." Evie turned to leave only to stop. "Actually, I wonder if you could give me Abigail's address."

∽

"What did I miss?" Tom asked as they crossed the street to the roadster.

"What do you mean?"

"You always seem to pick up on something obvious that escapes my notice."

"I didn't see anything unusual but I'm sure I'll experience some sort of delayed reaction." She only hoped it didn't happen when they were half way back to the house. She'd hate to have to return and make up some sort of excuse to drop in on Mrs. Green again. "I suppose if I think of something I could always contact the detective."

Evie stood by the motor car looking around. "Here's something I did notice. The villagers we encountered so far have gone about their business without showing any signs of dissent." The customers eating lunch at the pub hadn't been bothered by her presence. And, as if to prove her point, a woman strolled by, her attention on a storefront. When she saw Evie, she inclined her head slightly and continued on her way.

"Are we returning to Halton House now or do you wish to drop in on Abigail?"

"I have her address and we are already here, so we might as well pay her a visit."

They followed the directions Mrs. Green had given them and reached the end of lane. "This must be the cottage." The front window was open and Evie could see someone sitting at an angle as if to capture the light.

Tom knocked on the door. A young woman greeted them with a smile. When Evie introduced herself, Abigail bobbed a curtsey.

"Milady, I was just thinking about you. I've been

sitting here enjoying the sunshine and working on one of your gowns." She invited them inside her tidy cottage.

"I have only recently moved into the village so I'm still trying to make the place look like home." Abigail gestured toward a couple of chairs arranged in front of the fireplace.

"It looks very pretty."

"I'm still waiting for a few more pieces of furniture to arrive. My previous landlady looked after them until I could settle here. She'll be sending them soon..." Abigail jumped to her feet. "Where are my manners? Can I offer you some tea? Or would you like to look at one of your dresses?"

Evie knew she had missed her window of opportunity. She couldn't ask about her previous whereabouts without making it obvious. "Actually, I only wished to let you know you are welcome to come by Halton House, but I see you are quite comfortable working here. Although, now that I think about it, I do need to have a fitting. So... at your convenience, you could come by."

"Oh, I should like that very much, milady. I have never been inside a grand house."

"Then it's settled. We'll leave you to enjoy the sunshine." Evie waited until they had reached the end of the lane to say, "She looked quite happy working by the window."

"You didn't ask where she had lived before," Tom said.

"I tried to find the right moment. I suppose a detective would simply come straight out and ask." Evie lifted a shoulder. "Clearly, I'm not cut out to be a detective. Then again, I have invited her to visit Halton House, so there is still hope."

Tom held the passenger door open for her.

Evie climbed in and adjusted her hat. "I wonder how the detective would react to hearing from me so soon?" Would he take her seriously? Indeed, she had no idea if he had really decided to pursue the mad honey lead. For all she knew, he had only been humoring her. "I feel I should tell him about seeing Charlotte Davis riding away from the apiary. It might be important. I'll think about it some more and perhaps telephone him later in the day."

Tom put the motor car into gear and set off toward Halton House. "I suppose everyone will have finished their lunch by now."

"Since you mentioned it, I must admit I am feeling a little apprehensive. I find myself wondering what I will be returning to. At least Henrietta seems to be in a brighter mood." Evie tipped her hat up. "Is that Millicent walking on ahead?"

Tom slowed down.

"Yes, it is. Oh, do stop. She shouldn't have to walk the rest of the way."

Millicent heard them approaching and stopped to wait. "Milady! I'm ever so glad you stopped. I have been walking up and down the main street all morning and the prospect of walking back to Halton House had me wincing every step of the way."

"Why didn't you call the house and have Edmonds drive in to collect you?"

"I did call but Edmonds had gone to feed Mrs. Higgins' cat… you know, the one I'm supposed to be pretending to look after. I guess he hasn't returned yet and I couldn't wait to get back."

Tom climbed out and helped Millicent climb into the rumble seat.

"Hold on tight, Millicent," Evie warned.

"Oh, my. This is exciting."

As Tom drove off, Evie leaned over the seat and asked, "What did you find out?"

"As I said, I walked up and down. Oh… I saw the vicar. I must say, he is handsome."

Evie wondered if there was anyone Millicent didn't find handsome.

"We had lunch at the pub and saw him there," Evie said.

"That must have been soon after I saw him. This is such a pretty village. I couldn't help walking down some of the side lanes. Everyone takes such great care of their little gardens."

"Where exactly did you see him?" Evie asked.

"He was coming out of a cottage. He appeared to be in a hurry. I suppose being new to the village he is calling in on his parishioners and introducing himself. Oh, and then Anna Weston saw me in the village and dragged me back to her house for lunch."

"Dragged you? Did she physically force you to go with her?"

Millicent nodded. "She was fairly insistent. Meaning, she wouldn't take no for an answer. I suppose I should mention I felt reluctant to return to her house. What with not knowing if she is in full possession of her wits. Anyhow, I asked her about the honey and she took that as a hint to offer me some but, of course, I remembered you mentioning it this morning, so I refused because I didn't want to risk eating mad honey. If you want my opinion, I'd say she is in deep mourning for her friend and for the life she might have had if Mrs. Sheffield had introduced her to that special man. She went on about it for a while and then she brightened."

"Did something you said cheer her up?" Evie asked.

"Oh, no. Apparently, she has a man in her sights now. She's been baking up a storm because she thinks she needs to get some practice in for when she marries."

"Did she mention who this man is?"

"She says he gives her honey."

Evie exchanged a look with Tom that spoke of instant understanding. "Did she happen to mention his name?"

Millicent shook her head. "She said she wants to keep it a secret until she ties the knot. Apparently, someone else has her eye on him and Anna Weston is afraid of losing him to her competition." Millicent tilted her head in thought. "She said something about the other person now being free to pursue him, she would stop at nothing to get him."

What could that mean? Who else might be after a husband?

"You did very well, Millicent. Thank you." Evie straightened in her seat and thought about the Sheffield's beekeeper. Then she wondered about the other woman.

Could Mrs. Sheffield's sister be the woman Anna Weston feared would steal her beau?

"It makes sense," Evie said under her breath.

Chapter Twenty

As Tom helped Millicent down from the rumble seat, Millicent asked in a worried tone, "Would you like me to return to the village tomorrow, milady?"

Evie looked up and saw her maid's cheeks flushing a pretty shade of crimson. She didn't think it had anything to do with returning to the village. Turning, Evie saw Edgar standing by the porticoed entrance, his gaze fixed on Millicent. She couldn't quite make out his expression but she thought she detected a stern look.

Evie swung toward Millicent and saw her looking straight at Edgar.

Oh, dear.

Had Edgar caught Millicent's attention? Her maid loved flirting but that usually involved giggling and fluttering her eyelashes. Evie studied Millicent's face. Her cheeks remained flushed and she almost looked to be out of breath.

Oh, dear. *Oh, dear*.

Of all the men to be attracted to.

Edgar could be so proper at times, he might discourage Millicent and Evie didn't want to see her maid disheartened, or worse, heartbroken.

"I'm not sure there is anything more for you to find out in the village and I wouldn't want to put you in peril. For all we know, Anna Weston might be in the midst of some sort of emotional turmoil. We have already witnessed a display of her outburst. Who knows what she might do if you happen to say something she doesn't agree with."

Millicent breathed a sigh of relief. "As much as I have enjoyed the adventure, I must say I am not really cut out for this business. I suppose you will want me to return to town now." Millicent looked crestfallen.

"Oh, no... Not unless you don't want to," Evie assured her.

"But you already have a maid."

"Yes, but... Well, we have three guests who might need assistance and if you'd like to stay on here, I think we could find something else for you to occupy yourself with."

Millicent's eyes brightened. "That is the best news I have heard since you called to ask me to come here. Thank you, milady." Millicent bobbed a curtsey and took off on a light sprint leaving Evie and Tom to make their way to the front entrance.

"What was that about?" Tom asked.

Evie gave a woeful shake of her head. "In the course of averting a complication, I believe I have just somehow... managed to complicate matters." With Millicent free from her snooping duties in the village, she would spend more time at Halton House and that meant she would spend more time around Edgar.

"I see. Actually, I don't really and now I'm thinking the less I know, the better."

Edgar greeted them, "My lady. Mr. Winchester."

Evie smiled at him. "Edgar. Is there a particular room in the house I should avoid?"

Edgar looked puzzled.

Evie explained, "I wouldn't want to walk in on a rehearsal I'm not supposed to witness."

"Oh, I see." Edgar gave her a brisk smile. "Everyone is in the library and I believe they are eager to hear news from you."

"How is the play progressing?"

"It has hit a slight delay, milady. It seems the playwrights have floundered somewhat. They are experiencing some difficulties with motives."

"Greed is always a solid reason for murder," Evie suggested. "Revenge. Jealousy." Evie took off her hat and coat. As she handed them to a footman, she whispered under her breath, "Of course, there is also resentment." Evie brushed her hands across her face. "Heavens, just listen to me. When did I become an expert on motives for killing?"

Tom took her elbow and guided her toward the library. "I think you need to find a distraction or talk it through with the others."

She gave him a brisk smile. "There's an idea. Let's stoke the flames."

"Come on, the Countess of Woodridge doesn't drag her feet. Where's this reluctance coming from?"

"The thought of Mrs. Sheffield being killed has put me on edge. I think I'm almost afraid to discover the truth," Evie admitted.

They entered the library and found everyone slumped on their seats looking utterly bored. Seeing Evie and Tom, they all straightened, including Henrietta.

"Oh, Evangeline. We've been feeling rather lost without you."

Evie grimaced. "And you want to know what news I bring from the village?"

"That would be a good start." Henrietta turned toward the door where Edgar stood. "Edgar, I think we could all do with some tea."

"Certainly, my lady."

Henrietta patted the chair beside her. "Come and sit down and tell us everything that has happened."

Evie settled down and tried to organize her thoughts. So much had happened that morning. She glanced around and saw Tom moving toward his favorite spot by the fireplace. Grinning at her, he gave her a small nod of encouragement.

"Henrietta, why do you assume something has happened?" Evie gave a nervous laugh. "Fine, yes. Tom and I had a busy morning. But I am most interested in Millicent's tale so I will share that with you first. She had an encounter with Anna Weston. It appears she has her eye on someone and I'm thinking he might be Mr. Sheffield's beekeeper, Benjamin Nelson." As Evie explained about their visit to Mr. Sheffield's apiary and their encounter with his beekeeper, Benjamin Nelson, she wondered if Charlotte Davis should be included in the equation. It would certainly enhance the tale and Evie was sure the scriptwriters would appreciate it. Anna Weston had mentioned having competition and Evie couldn't think of a better candidate than Charlotte Davis…

"Go on," Henrietta encouraged.

Everyone shifted to the edge of their seats.

"Of course, it's nothing but wild speculation on my part, but I think there might be something to it. Anna Weston had hoped Mrs. Sheffield would introduce her to someone suitable." And then she had died, Evie thought.

Henrietta scoffed at the idea. "I doubt that woman had it in her to pave the way for anyone's happiness."

"Precisely," Evie said. "We know she enjoyed controlling people and I've been thinking of her as a queen bee. They're at the top of the food chain and only their well-being matters. In Mrs. Sheffield's case, someone else's happiness would only diminish her happiness."

Evie saw a few raised eyebrows. "Now that I think about it, she was probably the type to string people along with promises of happiness."

"I think she had other plans for you," Henrietta said.

Phillipa clicked her fingers. "She probably thought you were beyond her reach and far too content in your life. And... and she felt that cast a shadow on her life and, as you said, that would diminish her own happiness. So, she decided to bring you down a notch by making your life miserable."

Henrietta gave a pensive nod. "I have known a great many people who were not content to see others enjoying happiness. And don't get me started on those who take great joy in mistreating their servants. I have a pet theory about that. Let me think... it's something to do with a person's sense of self-worth and illusions of grandeur. They think they can only feel important by belittling others."

Evie got up and strode around the library.

"That's Evie's thinking walk. She is working through a theory," Phillipa said.

Humming under her breath, Evie stopped in the middle of the room. "This might be a far-fetched idea, but here goes. Anna Weston told Millicent she wants to get married and Mrs. Sheffield reneged on her offer to find her someone suitable. Anna Weston then went ahead and found someone herself but Mrs. Sheffield objected to her choice. A beekeeper would be too low in the social scale for someone of her acquaintance."

"You think Anna Weston killed Mrs. Sheffield as a way to stop her from disapproving?" Phillipa asked. "But why did she make such a scene when she came here to accuse the dowager?" Phillipa raised her hand. "Oh, I see."

"See what?" Henrietta asked.

"Anna Weston accused you of killing Mrs. Sheffield as a way of drawing attention away from herself," Phillipa explained.

"Let's run with the idea and fill in some gaps," Evie suggested. "Anna Weston is not getting any younger. This is probably her last chance at happiness. She has a roof over her head. But she's still lacking the one thing she wants the most. A husband. Who knows? Maybe she has actually fallen in love with the beekeeper. But how can she be happy with Mrs. Sheffield always around to criticize her choice?" Evie stopped to think about that. Had Mrs. Sheffield been that obsessive about her control over people? Evie turned to Henrietta. "How would you feel if I fell in love with a beekeeper and decided to marry him?"

Henrietta's eyes brightened. "My dear Evangeline. We already have honey. Could you not fall in love with a duke? Yes, I think that would be preferable."

"In other words, you would object to me falling in love with a beekeeper because in your eyes, he would always be a beekeeper."

"Well, think about it, Evangeline. What would you talk about during dinner? I think we would all soon tire of hearing about bees. I do wish you'd consider marrying a duke. Of course, that's not to say all dukes are engaging conversationalists. Heavens, I have met a few dull ones…"

When Evie sighed, Henrietta added, "I see, you actually wish me to object to the beekeeper. Yes, fine. I object."

"Thank you, Henrietta."

Henrietta tilted her head. "Does that mean you will now try to kill me so I won't stand in the way of your rather imperfect love match?"

"Yes, that's precisely what I might do."

"Oh, I now understand the point you were trying to make."

Tom brushed his hand across his chin. "Didn't Millicent mention someone else also had their eye on the beekeeper, or rather, on this mystery man Anna has found?"

"Yes. You read my mind and she actually said Anna Weston had competition from someone else," Evie said and turned to Henrietta. "We believe that person might be Charlotte Davis. We saw her riding her bicycle and we think she had been to visit the beekeeper. I don't know anything about her but I'm going to guess and say she is not married."

Now Henrietta looked confused. "Yes, but what does all that have to do with Mrs. Sheffield's death? Are you now saying there are two killers?"

"According to Evie's unsubstantiated theory," Phillipa said, "Mrs. Sheffield threatened to ruin their chances with the beekeeper and so they did away with her."

Evie didn't think both women had colluded to kill Mrs. Sheffield but… maybe one of them had.

"Perhaps including Charlotte Davis is too much of a long-shot." However, she thought Anna Weston made the perfect candidate. "We already know Anna Weston is inclined to act rashly," Evie mused.

"And you think she gave Mrs. Sheffield mad honey?" Tom asked. "Where would she get it from?"

That's for the police to find out, Evie thought.

The door to the library opened. Edgar stood aside and a footman entered carrying a large tray with a pot of tea and cups.

"I take it your theory has something to do with your foray into the village," Henrietta said. "What else did you discover?"

Evie gave a distracted nod as she sifted through the morning's events. Retracing her steps, she remembered they had gone to the dressmaker's store.

Why had Mrs. Green been in the store by herself? She hired servants. One would think she would organize them to help her clean up. "Oh," Evie exclaimed.

Phillipa clapped her hands. "Evie's had another bright idea."

"I just remembered. Mrs. Green gave a false account of Henrietta's altercation with Mrs. Sheffield. Why did she do that?"

"To throw everyone off her trail," Phillipa suggested and grinned. "I believe Evie has found another murder suspect."

Henrietta looked confused. "Are we now pointing the finger of suspicion at Mrs. Green? Who will make our gowns? She is the only dressmaker of note for miles around."

"We rather like the idea of Mrs. Green being the killer." Zelma Collins' remark prompted the other scriptwriters to nod in agreement. "And it ties in with what you already know. Mrs. Green's false statement to the police definitely makes her a person of interest."

Yes, but why would Mrs. Green want to kill Mrs. Sheffield? Evie took another turn of the room. "We need to find out everything we can about Mrs. Green's background."

Henrietta shifted. "We know she has lived in the village all her life."

"Do we know that for sure?" Evie asked.

"Yes, I can attest to the fact. Mrs. Green has been making my gowns for years."

"I suppose we also know she is happily married. So, her reasons for wanting to kill Mrs. Sheffield wouldn't be based on revenge."

"Actually… Mrs. Green is not married," Henrietta offered.

"What do you mean?" Evie laughed. "I'm sorry, I must sound so naïve." The housekeeper wasn't married and yet everyone knew her as Mrs. Arnold.

Henrietta helped herself to some tea. "Well, as far as I know, she has never married."

Zelma Collins cleared her throat. "If I may, I would like to apply your theory about Anna Weston to Mrs. Green. I believe it would work."

Bernie Peters murmured something in her ear.

"Oh, Bernie has an even better idea. It involves Mr. Sheffield."

Bernie nodded. "In her youth, before she became Mrs. Green, she might have been keen on Mr. Sheffield only to have him snatched from right under her nose by the woman who became Mrs. Sheffield."

"I like it." But how could they prove it? According to Henrietta, Mrs. Sheffield had grown up in the district. And Evie knew Mr. Sheffield had lived nearby. "It's quite possible they might have met at a young age."

Henrietta looked slightly lost. "I'm afraid you will have to spell it out for me."

Evie looked at Zelma and said, "Correct me if I'm wrong, we're thinking Mrs. Green met Mr. Sheffield many years ago. She had hoped to catch his attention and marry him but someone else beat her to it. And she has lived all these years regretting her missed opportunity. Then Mrs. Sheffield returned and took up residence in the village. The constant reminder of what might have been drove Mrs. Green to the edge of despair and she determined to do something about it."

Evie pictured the scene. Upon her return to the village, Mrs. Sheffield visited Mrs. Green's establishment and flaunted her marital status and good fortune. Mrs. Green endured it for as long as she could and then… She snapped.

"And if Mrs. Green gets away with murdering Mrs. Sheffield, will she then try to rekindle her lost love for Mr. Sheffield?" Henrietta asked.

"Yes, I think that's the idea."

"But what will you do?" Henrietta asked. "It seems unfair for the woman to have gone to so much trouble only to have her future plans ruined by someone who has figured out her evil plot."

"You'd like her to have a happy ending?" Evie smiled.

"The police might not reach the same conclusions you have, Evangeline. She still has a chance to get away with murder, make up for lost time and still continue to make our gowns."

Evie's eyes brightened with amusement. "Are you saying I should keep this information to myself?"

"Well, it is only conjecture on your part."

Evie spent the next ten minutes assuring Henrietta they had only been playing around with a plot idea for the play.

Or had they?

Chapter Twenty-One

Evie's head throbbed with too many theories and not enough explanations or facts.

She barely spared a glance at her surroundings as she made her way to her boudoir where she found Caro already preparing her bath.

"Where were you?" Evie asked. "You missed hearing all my theories as well as some new ones from the scriptwriters."

Caro folded a towel and set it down beside the bathtub. "Millicent was in a dreadful state, milady."

"Oh, what's happened to her? Is she ill?" Evie remembered Millicent had visited Anna Weston. Had she eaten some mad honey? No. She'd said she hadn't. "Did you call the doctor?"

"She's fine. Well, not exactly." Caro's shoulders lifted into a shrug. "It took me a while to get her to make sense. Finally, she admitted to being in love."

Evie visibly relaxed. "That's nothing new with Millicent. She's always falling for someone or other."

"This time it's different."

"How so?"

"She talked at great length about seeing someone every day and then suddenly, seeing them in a different light. Almost as if a veil had been lifted. At first, I thought it might be one of her infatuations but then she refused to eat anything for afternoon tea, which is unusual because Mrs. Horace baked her favorite lemon cake. I am afraid this is quite serious. Millicent never says no to lemon cake."

"Did she mention a name?" Evie asked even as a name popped into her head. *No, no, no. Not Edgar, please, not Edgar*. She couldn't be sure, but she thought she had once heard him describe Millicent as flighty.

Caro tested the water in the tub. "She made me guess and that took some time because I must admit I haven't been that observant and my mind has been elsewhere, rehearsing my lines for the play. So, I worked my way from one footman to the next."

"And?"

"And then I mentioned a few men from the village. She has been spending quite some time there so I thought she might have met someone new there."

Evie rubbed her temples. "Please tell me it's not Edgar."

Caro fell silent.

Evie shook her head. "Our girl cannot be infatuated with Edgar."

"I'm afraid it's worse than that, milady. She claims to be in love with him. She sounded convinced but I am prepared to wait until tomorrow. I'm thinking a good night's rest will do her a world of good. If not, I shall have to knock some sense into her."

"I hope a good night's rest will suffice," Evie murmured. "I'm not sure I could deal with a broken-hearted Millicent. Is there some way for you to find out if Edgar shares the sentiment?" She didn't wait for Caro to answer. "Do they even have anything in common? I would like to be open to the possibility but I'm having trouble picturing them together."

"It could be a case of opposites attracting," Caro offered. "Should we try to intervene or should we leave them to sort it out by themselves?"

Evie answered without hesitation. "No. We shouldn't interfere."

"You want to let nature take its course?" Caro sounded shocked. "But, anything could happen. What if something goes wrong? Their feelings are at stake. Not to mention our sanity."

"If something does go wrong," Evie said, "we will be there to support them." Evie wished she could find out how Edgar really felt about Millicent.

"Do you think we should try to throw them together as in… plan some sort of outing?" Caro asked.

"That sounds like a good idea but I would prefer to play it safe. Let them sort it out."

"So, you don't object."

"Why would I?"

Caro's eyebrows and voice hitched up in surprise. "Edgar is your butler."

"He's not my possession. The man is free to do as he pleases with his life."

Caro grinned. "So long as he doesn't look for another job."

"That's… That's different."

"Of course it is, milady. But what if Millicent's attention drives him away? Will you intervene then?"

Evie took a hard swallow. "They are both mature people. Well, most of the time. I think we can trust them to behave accordingly and, if things don't work out between them, then I'm sure they'll put it all behind them and... Oh, heavens. What if this is what drives Edgar away? And... And Millicent. What if it doesn't work out and she is so heartbroken she decides to move on? I don't want to lose either one of them."

Evie's legs crumbled from right under her and she sank into a chair. Suddenly, worrying about her granny's visit paled in comparison to what she would be forced to face if Edgar and Millicent left her.

She gave a firm nod. "Did I tell you about the theories you missed out on hearing? I think I would prefer to talk about Mrs. Sheffield's murder."

"Oh, so she was murdered."

Heavens. They still didn't know for sure.

~

"The more I think about it, the more I wonder about Mrs. Green," Tom remarked as he led Evie through to the dining room. "Despite the grievances we know Anna Weston harbored for Mrs. Sheffield because she failed to introduce her to a suitable man, Anna Weston put on quite a show when she interrupted our lunch. Can we really trust her? There might be something dreadfully wrong with her. She's almost too obvious to be the killer."

Evie agreed.

Tom continued, "Mrs. Green made the mistake of

contradicting the dowager's account. I wonder what she would say if we asked her to clarify what happened between Henrietta and Mrs. Sheffield?"

"We? Isn't this the part where you convince me to share the information with the detective and let him take care of it?"

"Yes, but I am contributing to what I hope will be a lively discussion. In the drawing room, I can fade into the background and avoid attention from the scriptwriters. It's a different story at the dinner table. So, I'm trying to get a head start. Besides, everyone seemed intent on pursuing your theories. I doubt they will wish to discuss anything else during dinner."

Again, Evie had to agree. The cocktail she had enjoyed just now had dulled her wits enough to prepare her for the next round of discussions. With any luck, she might be able to sit back and tune out.

The dinner table looked resplendent with an elaborate centerpiece arrangement and delicate spring blooms. Looking around the table, Evie only now noticed Tom was the only man joining them. Edgar had chosen to resume his duties and stood back to supervise the footmen. Evie almost wished the detective would barge in unannounced. Then she would be forced to invite him to dinner…

Evie looked across the table and smiled at Caro. She had asked her maid to join them thinking it would spare her the need to recount the evening's conversation.

Convincing Caro to accept an evening dress Evie hadn't worn since the previous season had taken some doing. In the end Caro had relented, laughing as she'd admitted she had felt compelled to put up a token resistance.

"Lady Carolina Thwaites looks resplendent," Tom mused.

Henrietta leaned in and said, "I was about to remark on her dress. I must say, it does look well on her."

Evie didn't know what to make of the remark. She knew Henrietta enjoyed baiting her, but she never employed malice. She turned toward Henrietta only to notice the dowager had changed her hair. If she mentioned it now, she would reveal the fact she hadn't noticed it before...

"Did you bring your maid with you?" Evie asked.

Henrietta smiled. "No, but your young Millicent has been quite helpful. I must say, she is very chatty. When she stopped talking, I looked up and realized she had completely changed my hair. It almost looks quite modern. Don't you agree?"

"Did she cut it?"

"No, she said it was all about styling. Did you know she is in love?"

"Heavens, what did she say?"

Henrietta laughed. "I'm really not sure. She did go on quite a bit. She said something about seeing a man in a new light. So, what do you think of my new style?"

"It's quite fetching and it suits you." Millicent had somehow managed to give the dowager a modern bob.

Glancing across the table, Evie noticed Phillipa looking surprised by something Zelma said.

"I wonder what that's about," Tom murmured.

Evie drew in a fortifying breath. "I believe we are about to find out."

"Everyone, Zelma has just come up with a most entertaining theory," Phillipa announced.

The young scriptwriter didn't need any encouragement. "We have been thinking about the new vicar. We'd spoken about making him a possible suspect by linking him to Mrs. Sheffield. Since they had both lived in London, we have decided the vicar must have had an affair with someone who now also lives in the village and that's why he has moved here."

"I must say," Henrietta whispered, "that sounds rather dull. You should help her out, Evangeline."

Zelma looked around the table and waited for someone to respond to her idea.

"This feels awkward," Tom whispered.

"Will you both please hush, she'll hear you," Evie whispered back.

Henrietta cleared her throat. "Do you have someone in mind for the vicar's love interest, Zelma?"

"No, I was rather hoping Lady Woodridge would be able to suggest someone."

Evie could think of two people who had recently arrived in the village. Mrs. Sheffield's sister and sister in law. They had been visiting for a number of weeks, but they resided elsewhere. If they had both lived in London, then it seemed possible for either one to have met the vicar. Then, she remembered Abigail...

Evie hoped she didn't live to regret making a suggestion. "I propose adding a new character based on Mrs. Sheffield's sister. She has never married because Mrs. Sheffield has objected to all her admirers. Determined to find some happiness, she has secretly been engaged to the vicar. When Mrs. Sheffield found out, she threatened to expose the vicar for some sort of scandalous wrongdoing. How am I doing so far? "

Zelma's lips parted. She looked around her. "Thank you, my lady. I knew our visit to Halton House would pay dividends. I hope you don't mind... I need a pen and paper."

"Perhaps you have missed your calling," Tom whispered.

Evie fell silent. She thought she had plucked the idea from out of nowhere. In reality, she couldn't stop thinking about Charlotte Davis.

Had the woman misled them by pretending to be in deep mourning? Did she have it in her to kill her sister? What would it take to drive someone into committing such a desperate act? Years of biting remarks and disapproval? False promises?

Evie's brief encounter with Charlotte Davis hadn't been enough to form an opinion about the woman's character but she'd seen enough to think of her as considerate and yet... she had been critical of her nieces for not hurrying to be by their father's side.

"Is there something wrong with your Salmon Mousse?" Henrietta asked.

"My apologies. I lost myself in introspection."

"I'm surprised you find the time. I must say, life will never be the same after this. Despite the circumstances, I have enjoyed coming to stay at Halton House. The last couple of days have been almost invigorating. You should plan a house party, Evangeline."

"You seem to forget my grandmother is about to descend upon us. I'm sure she will liven things up for us."

A footman strode up to Zelma and handed her some paper and a pen.

"My apologies, my lady. I really can't wait until we

retire to the drawing room to jot down the ideas you were so kind to provide."

"It's quite all right. I'm afraid I wouldn't be able to repeat them, so you should write them down while they are still fresh in your mind."

The footman took his place by Edgar's side and whispered something.

Evie saw Edgar's eyebrows curve upward. She set her fork down and sighed. "Edgar, has something happened?" And, if it had, she wondered if this would be the appropriate time to share the news. Evie felt torn between propriety and curiosity.

"As a matter of fact, yes, my lady. News has just reached the house courtesy of one of the footmen who just returned from the village. Mrs. Green's store has been broken into."

"Oh, heavens," Henrietta exclaimed. "It seems we are caught in a tempestuous upheaval. However, when all is said and done, I still maintain I will miss the excitement."

Chapter Twenty-Two

*E*vie wanted to close her eyes and picture a moment of peace and quiet. A time when she had been unburdened by other people's problems. Surely, she had felt carefree only a day or two before. She found herself staring at Edgar and he stared right back at her. When Evie tilted her head, he mirrored the motion.

She supposed he was waiting for a response or some sort of prompt from her.

"Does the footman have any other detailed information? Did he see the local constable on the scene? Were there local villagers congregated outside Mrs. Green's store?"

"No, my lady. He heard the news at the pub from someone who saw the police arrive."

"And how do we know it was a break-in?" And not another murder, she silently wondered.

"I believe the person relaying the information is related to the constable. You might say, he had inside information."

"This is going to be a long night," Tom murmured.

"Is there any way to confirm this really happened?" Phillipa asked. "Not that it matters, we'll find a way to work it into the play and that should keep us entertained until we learn more."

Zelma scribbled away, her meal all but forgotten. The others appeared to be waiting for someone to decide what to do. When, in fact, there was nothing for them to do, no action to take.

"Evangeline, I think they are all expecting you to make a statement."

Evie took a leisurely sip of her wine. As the hostess, her job was merely to ensure everyone felt comfortable and enjoyed themselves. She pondered the idea for a moment and accepted the fact her guests were sitting on the edge of their seats waiting for her to do or say something. "Mrs. Green's store has been closed since the incident. Perhaps... some hooligans decided to take advantage of the situation. I suppose we will have to wait until morning to hear more news." She couldn't send Millicent into the village. Evie turned to Tom and, lowering her voice, said, "I would welcome some input from you."

"Hooligans?" Henrietta could not have sounded more affronted. "I'm sure we do not have any hooligans in these parts. We might be besieged by the occasional poacher, but I doubt anyone wishing to trespass on private property has ever dared to set foot in our village."

"Poachers are a type of trespasser," Phillipa mused.

"There is a difference," Henrietta stated. "A poacher might climb over hedges but I dare anyone to claim a poacher would demean himself by breaking a window to enter a house."

"You sound offended, Henrietta," Tom teased.

"Yes, and I have every right to be," Henrietta said. "If we don't maintain some standards, where will we end up?"

"So, you're not offended by someone being murdered?" Tom asked.

Evie shifted her foot until she could be sure to land a swift kick.

Tom yelped. Recovering, he said, "Phillipa is right. The news will keep the scriptwriters entertained for the rest of the evening. You don't have anything to worry about." When Evie didn't respond, he smiled. "I guess that's not what you wanted to hear. I suppose we could go into the village tomorrow and snoop around. Since you visited Mrs. Green today to extend the offer of assistance, she might expect you to offer your moral support."

"Thank you. That's a sound idea. We'll call on her tomorrow morning. It will give us an opportunity to ask some pertinent questions. Can you think of any?"

"That depends. Is she still on your list of suspects?" Tom asked.

"I'm not sure I really have one of those." Evie reached for her glass again only to realize it was empty. "Could this be a case of Mrs. Green diverting attention from herself?"

Tom laughed. When Evie didn't join him, he said, "Oh, you're serious."

"Well, she did give a false account. Why did she contradict Henrietta? I know I keep asking that but only because there doesn't seem to be a reasonable explanation. We must find out who else witnessed the clash."

Tom leaned in and whispered, "What if she didn't contradict the dowager?"

"I heard that," Henrietta said. "Young man, I might be

old enough to be your grandmother but I still have full possession of my hearing."

Tom laughed.

"I see. You are teasing me." Henrietta turned her attention back to her meal only to say, "Or are you?"

"He is teasing you, Henrietta." Evie knew Henrietta would have no reason to lie. Mrs. Green's motivation, on the other, remained a mystery. Belatedly, she realized she'd had the perfect opportunity to ask Abigail about the altercation. They had all suspected there might have been a third person to witness the clash between Henrietta and Mrs. Sheffield. Had it been Abigail or one of the servants?

Heavens, and now there was the business of someone breaking in. What if it had been the killer, returning to the scene of the crime to remove evidence? Evie pulled herself away from that line of thought. It seemed senseless to wonder what other weapon might have been used against Mrs. Sheffield when they hadn't discounted the mad honey.

Scanning the table, Evie said, "I think we're ready to withdraw."

Henrietta chuckled. "And I think your prompt has become almost redundant. We have all finished, therefore, we will all withdraw to the drawing room. Unless, of course, Tom would like to remain here alone. Evangeline, you will have to organize yourself into collecting more male acquaintances to fill a few places at the table."

"I'm actually glad of the intimate setting," Evie admitted. "We can at least hope to contain the situation." She couldn't begin to imagine what an outsider would make of the scriptwriters using someone's misfortune to shape their story.

Henrietta's eyes sparkled. "I suppose this is not the best time to say Sarah telephoned earlier to inform me news had reached her about Mrs. Sheffield's death. She seemed to think you were somehow involved. I took great pleasure in putting her mind at rest by telling her all about my efforts to safeguard the family honor…"

∽

"Did you doze off?" Tom nudged Evie with his elbow. "If I have to sit through this, I think you could at least provide a distraction instead of sitting there playing Solitaire and dozing off."

"I had my eyes closed." And she had somehow managed to tune out of the conversations wafting around her. The scriptwriters had been reading the first act and had then asked for suggestions which Henrietta had happily provided.

Tom nudged her again. "Zelma Collins asked you a question."

Evie turned her attention to Zelma. "I'm sorry, I missed that."

"Which do you think would make more sense? Mrs. Sheffield discovering the vicar had a serious drinking problem or Mrs. Sheffield discovering he had asked for her sister's hand in marriage?"

Hadn't they decided to name the victim Mrs. Hatfield? And… Would she find a drinking problem scandalous? "I can't see why Mrs. Sheffield would disapprove of a vicar marrying her sister. He would give her sister respectability."

"Our next idea was to make the vicar promiscuous."

Really? Evie had trouble seeing the vicar as a *Lothario*.

Tom nodded. "He would be a perfect *Lothario*. Women would trust him."

"In my opinion, vicars need to be above reproach," Caro announced.

Evie sat up. She remembered Millicent saying she had seen the vicar coming out of a cottage. Why would that be unusual? Vicars visited parishioners all the time.

"You look as though you have just held an entire conversation with yourself," Tom observed.

"Yes, and I came close to arguing with myself and losing. Caro, could you please remind me to ask Millicent to describe the cottage? She'll know what it's about."

"Is this another theory in the making?" Tom asked.

Evie invited Tom to take a turn around the drawing room.

"I thought that only happened in Jane Austen books," Tom murmured.

"Oh, yes. The very books where heroes do a great deal of murmuring." Evie guided him toward the fireplace. "Let's pretend we're discussing the painting."

"I can't say I'm much of an art connoisseur. What can one possibly say about a pastoral scene?"

"That's perfectly fine. I only wish you to listen."

"Oh, yes. All men should be well trained in the art of listening." He smiled. "I'm all ears."

"I assume the detective will have spent the day interviewing the beekeeper and trying to find information about mad honey. What if he is missing someone obvious?"

"Are you referring to the vicar?"

Edgar cleared his throat.

Evie tensed.

"I always thought pastoral scenes were supposed to have a relaxing effect," Tom said. "You might not be looking at it properly. Your shoulders are as high as your ears."

Sighing, Evie turned. "What is it, Edgar?"

"I'm sorry to interrupt your… appreciation of one of Halton House's most treasured painting. I have just been informed the gamekeeper is at the kitchen door."

Evie knew the next question would determine how she spent the rest of the evening. If she asked it, she would no doubt spend the night tossing and turning. If she dismissed her curiosity, she would spend the night pacing. "Dare I ask, why? Did he encounter a poacher?"

"No, my lady. Or rather, he did encounter someone, but not a poacher. I thought you might want to discreetly exit the room."

"Edgar, thank you for your efforts. However, everyone is currently waiting with baited breaths to hear what you have to say to me. I will leave you to entertain them while Mr. Winchester and I go downstairs to investigate."

"Very well, my lady. I shall do my best."

As they walked out of the drawing room, Evie tapped her chin.

"Are you trying to remember something?" Tom asked.

"Yes, a word Henrietta used earlier. It describes our situation. Oh, yes. Besieged. Halton House seems to be besieged by strange happenings."

Tom's eyes sparkled with amusement. "It's almost as if you have become a magnet for murder and mayhem."

"It's no laughing matter, Tom. I'm thinking I should

abandon the idea of quiet days living in the country. It seems to be working in reverse for me." Evie stopped and grabbed hold of Tom's arm. "What if this is nothing but a ploy to get me out of the drawing room so they can work on their nefarious plan to get rid of me?"

"You?"

"Not me. My other me. My character in the play. They all seemed to be rather enthusiastic about it. Do you think that says something about the way the servants feel about me?"

"I'd prefer not to answer. At least, not until we reach the kitchen and see what this is all about."

Along the way, they encountered a couple of footmen in the process of clearing out the dining room. Most of the servants were hovering around the kitchen, clearly curious about the late-night visit.

"Edgar was not joking."

The gamekeeper stood by the end of the large kitchen table. Entering, Evie's attention went straight to the constable sitting at the table. And sitting opposite him...

"Detective?"

"My lady." The detective rose to his feet.

"Should I be worried about this?" Evie asked not quite sure if she should laugh as she realized there had been some sort of confusion.

The detective adjusted his tie. "Your gamekeeper escorted us to the house."

Evie turned to Mr. Ernest Rogers. "Is that so?"

"Aye, milady. I was making my rounds this evening when I came upon these two gentlemen. They were lurking in the woods. They looked suspicious and, to put it bluntly, they still do."

"Would someone please care to explain?" Evie asked. Turning to the detective, she gestured for him to follow. "Perhaps we might talk in the library."

The detective nodded and asked his constable to remain in the kitchen. "If that's all right with you, my lady."

"Yes, of course. Even in springtime it gets quite chilly outside. Perhaps Mrs. Horace might be kind enough to prepare a hot beverage?"

"At once, my lady."

Thanking the gamekeeper, Evie led the detective upstairs.

"I suppose you have a perfectly good explanation for lurking in the woods." She led him through to the library. "I wonder if your visit has something to do with Mrs. Green's store being broken into?"

"I see, you've heard about that."

Tom cleared his throat. "I think the Countess would really like to know what you were doing on her land."

"I was checking in on the constable. He has actually been stationed here for a couple of days."

"Without me being informed?" And the gamekeeper had only now found him?

"No one was supposed to know about him and he did a good job staying out of sight until tonight."

"May I ask why you took such measures?" Evie asked.

"At first, it was a precautionary measure. After Anna Weston's attack we thought it would be a good idea to keep an eye on the house. But now... Well, it appears you were right about the mad honey. Since you told me about it at the pub, I feared someone might have overheard you. The criminal mind is not something to be underestimated. I feared the person responsible might plan some sort of reprisal…"

Chapter Twenty-Three

She'd been right about the mad honey?

"What proof do you have about the mad honey?" Evie asked.

"I will spare you the details, my lady. However, an extensive post mortem examination has been carried out and it has now been confirmed Mrs. Sheffield had consumed large amounts of honey, possibly over a number of days, and a particular toxin has been found in her system. It should not have been enough to kill her but she had been suffering the symptoms of a weakened heart, something that surfaced only now."

He called that sparing her the details?

"Did her husband know about it?"

The detective shook his head "Mrs. Green had consulted a physician in London several months back. He had no knowledge of it."

Someone must have known about it…

The detective continued, "It is my understanding some honey was delivered to Mrs. Green's establishment."

Evie pressed a hand to her chest. "Pardon?"

The detective cleared his throat. "Mrs. Green said she received some honey from Halton House."

"Y-yes. That is correct. I organized it a couple of days ago. In fact, I asked my cook to organize a basket for the vicar too. Detective, are you suggesting my honey is responsible for Mrs. Sheffield's death? Impossible. I have been consuming that honey every day and you don't see me suffering from any strange symptoms."

He held her gaze for a moment before saying, "During the course of my investigation, I had the opportunity to speak with the vicar. He related an interesting account. It seems he overheard you making an admission and he described your behavior as odd. He also thought you looked quite hysterical."

Tom chuckled.

"Mr. Winchester, is there something you wish to say?" the detective asked.

"Yes, Tom. Do you wish to throw some light on the matter?" Evie asked.

"Oh, well…" Tom laughed again. "You really had to be there, detective, to understand the situation."

"Could you try to explain it, please?" the detective asked.

Tom's gaze slid over to Evie. "I had been teasing the Countess. In fact, I taunted her into playing a role. Unfortunately, the vicar overheard the Countess delivering a most convincing interpretation of a woman overcome by hysterics."

Evie huffed out a breath. "I cannot believe the vicar would misconstrue the situation. Nothing good is ever learned from eavesdropping. Frankly, I am shocked at the vicar's behavior. He should know better. If anyone should be accused of acting in an odd manner, it should be the vicar. He tried to run away."

The detective nodded. "That does sound odd. Then again, he had probably consumed some of your honey."

"Detective! I am shocked."

The detective brushed a hand across his face. "My apologies, my lady. It has been a long day."

Evie paced around the library. Frowning, she stopped. "Wait a minute. How did you connect Mrs. Sheffield's death to me giving Mrs. Green honey?"

"Ah, I wondered if you would notice. As you know, Mrs. Green's establishment was burgled tonight. When we informed Mrs. Green, she insisted on going to the store to see if anything of value had been taken. At first, she didn't notice anything missing. Then, she remembered her tea service which she had inherited from her grandmother. When she inspected the cupboard where she kept it in the small kitchen, she noticed a gap on the shelf."

"Someone took the honey," Evie said.

"Yes."

"And they probably think they have now removed the proof."

The detective nodded.

"Does that narrow things down?" Evie asked.

"Somewhat. After speaking with Mrs. Green, we now know Mrs. Sheffield became a regular visitor to her establishment. Mrs. Green was at first puzzled by the constancy of the visits. While Mrs. Sheffield had ordered some gowns, she had already been fitted for them. I suspect Mrs. Sheffield might have been waiting for someone else to put in an appearance."

Evie swung away and took a turn around the library. Henrietta had said she had felt as if Mrs. Sheffield had intended her to overhear her remarks. Had Mrs. Sheffield been waiting for Henrietta?

"Did Mrs. Sheffield use honey to sweeten her tea?" Evie asked.

"Yes, I established that after speaking with her sister, Charlotte Davis. And, yes, whenever she visited Mrs. Green's establishment, she drank tea sweetened with honey."

"So, how did that honey get there? Please don't say I supplied the mad honey. Did you speak with Benjamin Nelson? I don't wish to point fingers since he openly admitted rhododendrons and azaleas were best avoided around bees but someone must have supplied Mrs. Green with the mad honey."

The detective gave her a brisk smile. "As a matter of fact, Mrs. Green took your honey home with her."

"I see." Why had he waited until now to clarify that point? "Who brought the mad honey to Mrs. Green's establishment?" Evie sat down. Her gaze jumped from Tom to the detective. "Actually, did you ever find out where mad honey can be purchased from?"

The detective drew out his notebook, glanced at it and then put it away. "There are a number of questionable establishments in London catering to clients seeking… alternative methods…"

Not wishing to hear more, Evie held a hand up to stop him.

"We are still looking into identifying a buyer. London police is working on it."

"Do you have any theories about who might have

broken into Mrs. Green's store?" Evie clicked her fingers. "My maid spoke with Anna Weston today. She has her eye on a new man and she said he has been supplying her with honey. Perhaps you might want to speak with her. Now that I think about it, Anna Weston's behavior is odd enough to suggest she might have been consuming mad honey. Since you've had a constable keeping a close watch on Halton House, I suppose we can all breathe easy."

"Our investigation is still on-going, my lady." He checked the time. "It's getting late. Please accept my apologies. I hope you were not greatly alarmed."

"Before you leave… How did Mrs. Green react to the news her store had been broken into?"

"Shocked. Why do you ask?"

"Is it possible she might have faked a break-in?"

"Why would she do that?" The detective dropped his gaze and smiled. "I see. You think she is trying to lead the police away from her trail. You actually suspect her."

Evie glanced at Tom. "Well… We have been tossing around a few ideas and they include Mrs. Green seeking revenge."

"Revenge? Over what?"

"It's rather complicated." Evie sighed. "Is there a way to establish Mrs. Green's whereabouts tonight?"

"Yes, we found her at home. She had a visitor."

"Oh. I see."

"Did you really think she had broken into her own store?" The detective tilted his head. "Tell me about your theory regarding Mrs. Green seeking revenge."

Seeing the detective's eyes sparkling with amusement, Evie lifted her chin. "We've had reason to suspect Mrs. Green. After all, she gave a different account of the dowager's confrontation with Mrs. Sheffield. Anyhow… As a young woman, before she became Mrs. Green, she had been besotted with a young man… Mr. Sheffield. And…"

The detective smiled and shook his head. "And you think Mrs. Sheffield stole him away from Mrs. Green."

"Yes."

The detective went on to summarize the plot almost as if he had eavesdropped on the scriptwriters. He shrugged. "It actually doesn't sound that far-fetched. I've heard more ludicrous excuses for murder."

"Here's another theory we have been playing with. Again, I don't wish to point fingers… Charlotte Davis, Mrs. Sheffield's sister. We saw her riding her bicycle and we're almost certain she visited the beekeeper."

The detective sighed. "I've had a constable watching the Sheffield house. No one left tonight. So, she didn't have anything to do with the theft of the honey."

Not directly, Evie thought. "Do you have the entire village under surveillance?"

"Only those people we suspect."

Evie had to remind herself he'd had someone keeping an eye on Halton House because of a possible threat from Anna Weston.

Seeing the detective rise to his feet, Evie scrambled to find something else to ask him before he left. "How… How will you follow up on the honey theft? The thief must surely be involved in killing Mrs. Sheffield. Or maybe someone hired the thief…"

"Well…" The detective tilted his head.

"What? Did you just think of something?" Evie asked.

"Yes, as a matter of fact, I have. Thank you."

"Oh, was it something I said?"

"Yes. We might be looking for more than one person. You said the thief might have been hired to break in…"

Smiling, Evie said, "Oh, right… I'd like to claim I knew what I was talking about, but I'm afraid I just said the first thing that came to mind."

"Detective O'Neill warned me about that. You really don't give yourself much credit."

"I'll send a footman down to alert the constable."

When the detective left, Evie sighed. "I'm really hoping there is an end in sight." She nibbled the tip of her thumb.

"Dare I ask? What are you thinking about?" Tom asked.

"The vicar. Did he try to point the finger of suspicion at me?"

Tom sat down beside her and mused, "The scriptwriters made the vicar a suspect."

Evie exclaimed. "We should suggest they make him the killer."

"You only say that because you don't want Evie Parker to be responsible for the fictional Mrs. Sheffield's death."

"As a matter of fact, I don't think my character has it in her to kill anyone. She's been rescued from the poorhouse and most likely feels indebted. Why would she bring the family name into disrepute?"

"I think you make a valid point. But what possible reason would the vicar have for killing Mrs. Sheffield? Oh, wait. The scriptwriters decided he had known Mrs. Sheffield in London."

Evie straightened. "Hang on. I remember Phillipa saying a scandal drove him to the countryside and Mrs. Sheffield is the only one who knows about it."

Tom nodded. "Yes, but that's fiction. If there had been a scandal, the detective would know all about it by now. I'm sure he has looked into everyone's background."

True.

Evie surged to her feet and walked to the door. Peering out into the hall she saw a footman. "Could you ask Millicent to come to the library, please?"

Sitting down again, she tried to separate fact from fiction. "That play is playing havoc with my mind."

Moments later, Millicent came in. "Milady? You asked to see me?"

"Oh, Millicent. Yes, come in."

Millicent brushed her hand along her dress.

"Do sit down."

Her maid sat on the edge of a chair.

"Do you remember telling us about seeing the vicar in the village?"

"Let me think. Oh, yes. I said I had been wandering around the village."

"And you saw him coming out of a cottage."

"Yes."

"Can you describe the cottage?"

"It's at the end of a lane. It has a couple of pretty shrubs. I think they might be lavender. I didn't get close enough to see."

"And you're sure the vicar came out of the cottage."

Millicent nodded. "Yes, and he appeared to be in a hurry but then he slowed down his step. Almost as if he didn't wish to be seen coming out of the cottage but once he'd put some distance, he probably wanted to appear to be out and about."

Tom looked at her. "Abigail's cottage?"

"Yes, I think so." Both Abigail and the vicar were new to the village and, despite what Abigail had claimed, they knew she had been living in London. How could they confirm it?

"Thank you, Millicent."

"Have you come up with a plot to rival the scriptwriters' outlandish plot?" Tom asked.

"I think I have. But we'll have to speak with the detective first. That can wait until tomorrow. Shall we join the others? I think they'll wish to hear about this conversation…"

Chapter Twenty-Four

*E*vie removed her gardening gloves and handed them to a footman. She had managed to avoid everyone for an entire morning by having breakfast in her room and then taking refuge in the garden. Not even Tom had approached her. Although, she knew he had arrived at the house in time for breakfast.

"Ah, Evangeline. There you are… My heavens, you look very earthy." Henrietta brushed a finger against her cheek.

"I suppose I have dirt on my face again. Was there something you wished to see me about, Henrietta?"

"Well, yes. You have missed this morning's rehearsal. After everything you told us last night, the scriptwriters have been quite busy rewriting some scenes." Henrietta looked over her shoulder and lowered her voice. "They have decided to turn you into a red herring."

"Oh. I see."

"Surely, you could show more gratitude."

"Yes, I suppose so. Actually, which part did they find

most intriguing?" She couldn't remember making that much sense. After the detective had left, she and Tom had rejoined her guests and had given them a brief summary of their conversation with the detective. Evie remembered their puzzled expressions when she had corrected Tom and then Tom had corrected her. They had eventually settled on the right information. In actual fact, Evie believed the detective had merely been humoring her.

How could two people be involved in killing Mrs. Sheffield?

"They were most intrigued by the connection between the vicar and Anna Weston, of course," Henrietta said.

"Oh, right…" Evie searched her memory and finally remembered the scriptwriters had settled on Anna Weston as a main suspect instead of Abigail. "To tell you the truth, I'm still not convinced and if I'm not convinced then the audience watching the play won't be convinced." Evie sighed. "I'm sorry, Henrietta. I have been out in the sun too long and I wish to change out of these clothes."

"Can we expect you sometime soon?"

"Yes, of course. I'll be with you shortly." She supposed she could sit in a corner and play a game of Solitaire. If the scriptwriters had chosen someone else as their killer then she wouldn't have much of a role to play.

Evie made her way up the stairs, her thoughts engaged on trying to remember exactly what she had said the night before to change everyone's mind. She had mentioned Anna Weston and Charlotte Davis.

Two women in love with the vicar…

When she reached the landing, Evie heard footsteps crossing the entrance hall. Looking down, she saw Tom. "Hello, where have you been?" she called down.

Seeing her, Tom made his way up the stairs. "I went into the village to see if I could find the detective. After last night's discussion, I wanted to ask if he had looked into the vicar's background."

Evie could not have looked more surprised. "You have actually gone out of your way to seek information? You usually try to talk me out of becoming involved…"

"Actually, it was all I could think of doing to get out of the house. The scriptwriters were ganging up on me. I thought they had given up, but they appear to be more determined than ever to rope me in."

"So, did you learn anything new?"

"Yes, I caught up with the detective at the pub. He's been staying there." He nodded. "The vicar and Mrs. Sheffield had been acquainted when they both lived in London but the detective didn't discover any scandals."

That meant the vicar wouldn't have a reason to kill Mrs. Sheffield. Unless, he had shown an interest in her sister, Charlotte Davis. "And he hasn't been able to connect them to anyone else?"

"No. He said he would be talking to Anna Weston again this morning. He wants her to reveal the identity of the man who's been giving her honey."

Good luck with that, Evie thought. "Give me ten minutes to prepare. I would like to go to the village."

"Ten minutes?"

"Fine… Twenty minutes."

Tom tapped his cheek.

"Okay. Make it half an hour." When she reached her room, she found Millicent in there tidying up.

"Milady. Caro suggested I might make myself useful here since she is busy rehearsing."

"You don't seem to be happy about that, Millicent." Evie realized she'd spoken too soon. She guessed Millicent's downcast expression didn't have anything to do with missing out on the play, but a great deal to do with her infatuation with Edgar.

"It must be the sunshine, milady. I always feel this time of the year inspires great love of everything but not everyone is willing to feel the same way."

Oh, dear.

Had Edgar already put her in her place?

"Perhaps you need a distraction," Evie suggested. "Would you like to come to the village with us? Tom and I are planning a trip there this morning."

Millicent appeared to give the offer some thought and then she brightened. "That would be fantastic, milady. Yes, please. Are you going to spy on someone?"

Evie wanted to say she thought it was time to start asking some tough questions but she didn't think she would sound convincing enough. "I think I should pay Mrs. Green a visit and offer my support. Oh, now that I think of it, it would be nice to take her a basket. Could you organize that with Mrs. Horace, please. But first, let's find a suitable dress for the outing. Something cheerful."

Half an hour later, they both descended down the stairs and hurried outside to meet Tom who stood waiting by the roadster.

"We have company," Evie said

Tom took the small basket from Millicent and helped her settle into the rumble seat. Handing her the small basket, he asked Evie, "Are you going to bribe someone?"

"I'm merely going to extend my offer of support. I thought Mrs. Green would appreciate a basket."

"She might," Tom agreed. "Then again, she might have heard about the mad honey and think you were trying to poison her."

A short while later, they arrived in the village and Tom asked, "Which way?"

"Oh. How remiss of me. I have no idea where Mrs. Green lives." Evie turned around and asked, "Millicent, do you happen to know where Mrs. Green lives?"

"I'm ever so sorry, milady. I don't."

Straightening, Evie gestured with her hand. "Drive on, Tom. We'll pay Abigail a visit. She might be able to give us Mrs. Green's address."

As soon as they turned into the lane, Millicent gasped. "This is where I saw the vicar. He came rushing out of that cottage at the end of the lane." She pointed ahead at Abigail's cottage.

"Well, it seems we have made a connection," Evie murmured. But, what did it mean?

Abigail had her window open and Evie could see her once again sitting by the window with her sewing in hand.

"I almost don't wish to interrupt her. That looks like one of my gown," Evie whispered.

Ignoring her, Tom went ahead and knocked on the front door.

Evie watched Abigail set her sewing down and peer out the window. Seeing her, she rushed away and a second later the front door opened.

"Milady. What a surprise."

"Good morning, Abigail." Evie held up the small basket she had intended giving to Mrs. Green. "We brought you a basket."

"Oh, how lovely."

Instead of reaching for the basket, Abigail hesitated. In fact, Evie noticed she kept her hands out of sight.

"Would you like me to set it down somewhere?" Evie asked and took a step forward.

Abigail reached out to take the basket and again hesitated.

"Abigail! My goodness. You've cut your hand." Evie took another decisive step inside the cottage while at the same time, Tom grabbed hold of her arm and pulled her back.

"It's… it's nothing, milady. I was clumsy with the scissors."

As Tom tugged Evie back again, Millicent took advantage of the gap and dove inside, pushing Abigail back.

"Millicent!"

"Milady. She's cut her hand. Don't you see what that means?"

"Yes, I do. Now, please step aside." Turning to Abigail, she said, "It looks like a bad cut."

Abigail cradled her injured hand. "It's really nothing but a scratch, milady."

"Yes, I see. And how exactly did you happen to scratch your hand with a pair of scissors? Did a broken piece of glass have anything to do with it?"

Abigail's mouth gaped open. She jumped back but then stilled as if in shock.

"Is there something you wish to tell us, Abigail?"

"If not us, then the detective," Millicent said. "Yes, I'm sure the detective would be greatly interested in her story. Clearly, she cut herself while breaking into Mrs. Green's store." Millicent wagged a finger at Abigail. "If you tell the truth, they'll go easy on you. Why did you kill Mrs. Sheffield?"

"B-but… I didn't."

The distant sound of sirens had them all tensing.

"They're coming to get you," Millicent warned.

"But I didn't do anything. I mean…"

"Evie," Tom warned.

"She won't do anything." Evie turned to Abigail. "Isn't that right, Abigail?"

The young woman gave a shaky nod.

"Evie!" Tom warned again.

"You broke into the store to get the honey," Evie said.

Abigail's lip wobbled. Finally, she gave a small nod. "I had to. I didn't know it was bad. He… he never told me. But after everything that's happened, I thought the police would find out I brought the honey to the store. But he gave it to me…"

"He? You mean, the new vicar." It had to be.

"He said Mrs. Sheffield loved honey. He's a vicar. Why would he want to kill Mrs. Sheffield?"

After that confession Abigail clammed up and it took some doing to get her to talk and tell them the rest.

When she finally told them the whole story, Evie took Tom aside. "Someone must alert the detective but we can't leave Abigail alone. You stay here with Millicent."

"What? No. Absolutely not."

"It makes sense," Evie insisted. "I'll be safe. I can't send you or Millicent. If the vicar decides to do something, you'll be here to protect Abigail. He wouldn't think of assaulting me."

"What makes you think the detective hasn't already figured it all out?" Tom asked.

"Because he's not here. If the vicar had confessed, he would have involved Abigail." Not wanting to argue the point any further, Evie walked out of the cottage, leaving Tom to grumble and threaten to tell her grandmother about her scandalous antics.

As Evie made her way to the heart of the village, Evie thought about the vicar visiting Abigail to tell her there might have been something wrong with the honey. That meant he must have overheard them talking at the pub.

Evie wished Abigail had chosen to tell the police instead of panicking and deciding to remove the honey herself. It wouldn't look good for her…

Once Evie reached the corner, she scanned the street, keeping an eye out for the detective. He had to be around somewhere. The night before, he'd said he planned on talking with Anna Weston. Her house was only a short distance away, not far from the vicarage.

Evie hurried her step. When she caught sight of the vicar's house, she knew she had to turn the corner but then she saw the police motor car.

Outside the vicar's house!

Clearly, the detective had made the connection. Had he spoken with Abigail? He couldn't have. Otherwise, Abigail would have mentioned it.

After her initial hesitation, Abigail had been quite talkative, saying the vicar had wanted to do anything he could to please Mrs. Sheffield because when he'd lived in London he had fallen in love with her sister and wanted Mrs. Sheffield to approve of the match.

But the vicar had clearly had other ideas, Evie thought…

He'd wanted to get rid of Mrs. Sheffield who had no

doubt objected to the match between him and Charlotte Davis.

Evie hurried toward the vicarage but as she drew nearer, her steps slowed.

Why hadn't the vicar just given the honey to Mrs. Sheffield himself? Why had he taken the trouble of hiding the fact the honey had come from him by enlisting Abigail's help?

"Of course. He knew the honey would have an adverse effect," Evie murmured. And when Mrs. Sheffield died, the finger of suspicion would have been pointed at him without delay.

Had he really known?

Evie saw the detective emerging from the vicarage with the vicar. He had his hand clasped around the vicar's arm and was leading him to the police motor car.

The vicar looked red-faced but he didn't appear to be struggling.

Would an innocent man protest his arrest or would he think everything would eventually be sorted out?

The detective saw Evie. He spoke to a constable and put him in charge of the vicar so he could approach Evie.

"Lady Woodridge."

"Detective. I see you have made an arrest."

"Yes, finally."

"What about Abigail?" Evie asked.

"What about her?"

"Didn't the vicar try to embroil her in the plan to kill Mrs. Sheffield?"

The detective looked puzzled. "Why would he do that?"

"Are you saying the vicar didn't mention Abigail at all?"

"No, he didn't."

That didn't make sense. "Did he tell you where he got the honey from?"

"Not yet. But he will."

It had taken a little research to discover the effects of mad honey. Had the vicar been aware of what it would do to someone with a weakened heart?

How would he know about Mrs. Sheffield's condition? It hadn't been common knowledge.

Evie gasped. "Charlotte Davis would have known."

"Pardon?"

"Mrs. Sheffield's sister would have known about her condition." Charlotte would also know her sister well enough to realize she would never approve of the vicar. Not because there was anything wrong with him, but simply because... Well, they had already decided Mrs. Sheffield loved to make other people miserable with her petty criticisms. "Detective, this might sound like a strange question."

The detective looked over his shoulder and then back at Evie. "I have a few moments. What is on your mind, my lady?"

"We know Mrs. Sheffield inherited the house and the land. Did she retain ownership of it and who inherits it upon her death?" Evie knew the police must have looked into possible motives, among them, financial gain. "Detective, I believe the vicar will eventually confess to receiving the honey from Miss Charlotte Davis."

Epilogue

"I'm not sure about this color." Evie stood in front of the mirror scrutinizing her new gown. "Yellow doesn't really suit me."

"It's not really yellow, milady." Caro adjusted the sleeves. "I think it's closer to mustard."

"I'm wearing the color of a condiment?"

"This shawl complements it beautifully."

"I still feel I'm fading into the background."

Caro pinched her cheeks.

"Ouch!"

"You just need a little color on your cheeks. There, that's done the trick. You look quite cheerful now, in a grim sort of way. You should be quite pleased with yourself, milady. You helped the police find the real killer."

And yet, she couldn't find pleasure in that. The vicar had been cleared of all wrongdoing while the real culprit awaited trial.

Evie tried smiling. "Is that better?"

"Much better." Caro stepped away and busied herself gathering Evie's floral pattern dresses. "I'm ever so grateful for these dresses, milady. They are so pretty. I shall have to plan outings for every Sunday until the end of days."

"I'm glad you like them. You can still have something new made. Perhaps something in a bold shade."

"Oh, but I rather like the floral patterns, milady."

"Nevertheless, Mrs. Green is expecting you."

"I hope you don't mind me saying so, milady, but Mrs. Green had a close call. She's lucky to still have you as a client. After all, she gave the police a conflicting report which made the dowager look bad."

Yes, but poor Mrs. Green had been under the influence of mad honey too…

Evie cast a forlorn glance at the dresses. She had a wardrobe full of new gowns, all in bold colors, with more on the way because she had promised to give Mrs. Green more work to make up for the customers she had lost. Toodles would definitely approve.

Time to move on, she thought.

"I think I'm as ready as I will ever be."

"Have you been rehearsing your lines?" Caro asked.

Evie nodded. "I'm sure I have been practicing them in my sleep. These last few days I have been waking up with a dry throat." Evie turned and glanced at her reflection. "I'm not sure this is the right dress to wear. After all, I am playing the role of a poor relation rescued from the poorhouse."

"But at least you won't be the killer."

"Do you think the scriptwriters will change their

minds?" Evie asked. "It doesn't quite seem right to base their story on fact."

"If you ask me, that woman had it coming. If she'd wanted to marry the vicar, she should have eloped. But, oh no… she wanted to inherit the money as well. That's greedy. I would have been content to find a good husband."

"Is that what you want, Caro?"

Caro tilted her head from side to side. "Eventually."

Picking up the hat Caro had chosen for her, she tried it on. Sighing, Evie asked. "What about Millicent? Do we have any news about her infatuation?"

Caro grinned. "As a matter of fact, Mrs. Horace was rather busy this morning preparing a basket for Edgar and Millicent. They are going on a picnic this afternoon."

Evie swung around. "Really?" Her smile faded. "Wait. Should I be concerned?"

Caro shook her head. "They both look happy. Edgar has been walking around rehearsing his lines and smiling like a giddy school boy."

"Do we know how it happened? Did he ask her out or did Millicent take the plunge?"

Caro laughed. "Millicent gave him an ultimatum. She cornered him and said she was too old-fashioned to ask him out and he should be man enough to do it. So, she said she would wait until he decided what he wanted to do but he should hurry up because there were plenty of fish in the sea and she had no intention of waiting around forever, but she would give him a month or so. After which time she would definitely start looking elsewhere."

"She said all that?"

"And then some. By the time Millicent finished giving Edgar a piece of her mind, he had made up his mind to just get it over and done with and he told her so. Then, he said it would be a shame to start on such a wrong foot so he would wait a day for the dust to settle and then ask her out because he wanted to and not because she had forced his hand. They both put on quite a show."

"I really hope it all works out for them." And since she had asked Millicent to stay on at Halton House, Edgar would also stay on. Evie's smile brightened.

Caro stood back and asked Evie to turn around for a final inspection. "What I don't understand is why Abigail agreed to sneak the honey in. She should have been more suspicious."

Evie agreed. "The same could be said about the vicar. He should have been suspicious of Charlotte Davis instead of believing the honey would please Mrs. Sheffield no end. Anyway, Abigail said she was afraid of losing her position." Evie tapped her finger against her chin. "Heavens, I think I've forgotten all my lines."

"You can't have. You're so bright, milady. You even knew Charlotte Davis was up no good because you saw her riding away from the apiary." Caro shook her head. "Such a bad apple. Just like her sister who couldn't stand for anyone to be happy. Actually, Charlotte was worse than her sister and proved it when she went out of her way to interfere with the blossoming love between the beekeeper and Anna Weston."

Yes, a bad apple indeed.

"Yellow," Evie shook her head. "Caro, you'd tell me if the color isn't right for me."

"Of course. I would never hesitate. Even at the risk of it sounding like criticism. My mother taught me better than to be petty and critical. She always says such behavior says more about the person than anything else. So, I would employ the utmost discretion. And, for the record, I don't mind that you're American."

"Heavens, I'd almost forgotten Mrs. Sheffield had also criticized me for that."

"I've spoken with a few villagers," Caro continued, "and they all reported Mrs. Sheffield had been a tad harsh with quite a few of them. To think this all started with Mrs. Sheffield's petty criticism."

"Oh, but it started long before then," Evie said and turned to study her reflection. Charlotte Davis had been plotting to get rid of her ever so critical sister for a long time. Or at least since learning of Mrs. Sheffield's weakened heart. To think she had used her sister's weakness for honey against her.

"Do we know if Charlotte Davis gave Anna Weston mad honey?" Caro asked as she adjusted Evie's hat. "It would certainly account for the woman's odd behavior."

"Yes. I forgot to tell you. The detective said Charlotte Davis confessed to leaving a pot of honey outside Anna Weston's house. She played on the woman's vulnerability by making her think it had come from the beekeeper. I must say, she was quite cunning, killing two birds with one stone. Charlotte Davis knew her sister had been a regular visitor and so she used the opportunity to expose her to more mad honey.

"Well, I'm glad it's over. Now we have your grandmother's visit to look forward to."

Evie's shoulders hitched up.

Laughing, Caro rested her hands on Evie's shoulders. "You should take a deep breath now, milady."

"Thank you for the reminder." Evie scooped in a breath. "I'm ready if you are. As they say, the show must go on."

∽

Author Notes

All care has been taken to remain historically correct. Normally, I include a list of words or phrases which had been in use well before the 1920s. This time, however, I am only including one. The phrase does not appear in this story because the phrase came into use in 1939

The penny drops

The Oxford English Dictionary states that this phrase originated by way of allusion to the mechanism of penny-in-the-slot machines. The earliest citation of a use of the phrase with the 'now I understand' meaning, is from The Daily Mirror August 1939

Printed in Great Britain
by Amazon